Murder in Melucha

Read the first book in the series by Aditi Krishnakumar
The Magicians of Madh

Read more for young adults from Duckbill
The Lies We Tell by Himanjali Sankar
Talking of Muskaan by Himanjali Sankar
Zombiestan by Mainak Dhar
Jobless Clueless Reckless by Revathi Suresh
Facebook Phantom by Suzanne Sangi
The Right Kind of Dog by Adil Jussawalla
Shiva & the Rise of the Shadows by Kanika Dhillon
The Wordkeepers by Jash Sen
Skyserpents by Jash Sen
Daddy Come Lately by Rupa Gulab
Unbroken by Nandhika Nambi
When She Went Away by Andaleeb Wajid
Invisible People by Harsh Mander
Wanting Mor by Rukhsana Khan
When Morning Comes by Arushi Raina
Year of the Weeds by Siddhartha Sarma
Queen of Earth by Devika Rangachari
Queen of Ice by Devika Rangachari

Murder in Melucha

In which the story progresses from Madh to Melucha

Aditi Krishnakumar

duckbill

An imprint of Penguin Random House

To J, who likes murder mysteries.

DUCKBILL BOOKS

USA | Canada | UK | Ireland | Australia
New Zealand | India | South Africa | China

Duckbill Books is part of the Penguin Random House group of companies whose addresses can be found at global.penguinrandomhouse.com

Published by Penguin Random House India Pvt. Ltd
7th Floor, Infinity Tower C, DLF Cyber City,
Gurgaon 122 002, Haryana, India

Penguin Random House India

First published in Duckbill Books by
Penguin Random House India 2021

10 9 8 7 6 5 4 3 2 1

ISBN 9780143451969

Typeset in Sitka by PrePSol Enterprises Pvt. Ltd
Printed at Replika Press Pvt. Ltd, India

www.penguin.co.in

FSC www.fsc.org MIX Paper from responsible sources FSC® C016779

Prologue

The story begins with a young prince. He stood in the doorway to his study, very carefully *not* screaming. In a pool of lamplight on the floor, a cobra swayed with its hood flared, glittering eyes never leaving the prince's face.

His first instinct was to use magic to trap the snake. His fingertips tingled with the urge—but he didn't dare. His position was still precarious. If the spell went wrong . . .

He weighed his options.

Fortunately, he was wearing slippers of hard leather, which were covered in mirrorwork and gold embroidery. They were uncomfortable. They squeezed his feet and made his toes itch. They were bad for running. But they were good protection against such common dangers of Melucha as snake fangs.

Less fortunately, the slippers ended at his ankles and his leggings were of soft silk.

'A cobra won't strike with its hood up,' he said under his breath, repeating a lesson he'd learnt from his tutor several years ago, and fervently hoping that it was more accurate than Kras's lessons usually were. 'Stay calm, make no loud noises, back away slowly and call the safety team for disposal.'

He stayed calm—outwardly, at least.

He made no loud noises.

He began to back away into the dim corridor.

Before he could call the safety team, he tripped over the door frame and fell to the ground, jarring his elbow. A streak of dark lightning shot towards him out of the pool of light, and now he couldn't *see* it—

There was a flash of movement beside him. Something clattered, something clinked and the cobra hissed.

'Really, Kalban,' said an exasperated voice. 'There's a snake hook by the door. There always is. There's no need to *panic*.'

Footsteps went to the window. As they passed by the lamp, Kalban saw that his younger brother Abhinav had the wriggling snake trapped in the blunt hook.

'There.' He opened the window, dropped the snake outside, and shut it again.

'What about the gardeners?'

'Gardeners who don't know what to do when they see a cobra don't have good career prospects in Melucha.'

Unspoken was that *princes* who didn't know what to do when they saw a cobra didn't have good career prospects in Melucha, either. Or, for that matter, good life expectancy.

'I had all the same lessons you did,' Kalban muttered, getting to his feet.

'Yes, so any difference in how we respond to everyday situations can be attributed to my superior natural intelligence. Did you learn *anything* useful in Madh?'

Kalban snapped his fingers. Lamps around the room flared to life.

'Very impressive,' said his brother, in a tone that conveyed the opposite. 'If the city lamplighter ever wants to retire, we know who can take over. Are you all right now? Or do you want me to stand here while you open your letters, in case one of them has a poisoned needle?'

'I'm fine,' Kalban snapped.

'Please yourself. I'll just come back if I hear you screaming, shall I?' He dropped the snake hook on the desk. 'You'd better get some practice with this.'

'I *didn't* scream,' Kalban said to his brother's retreating back. Then he sighed. As little as he liked to admit it, his reflexes had . . . well, not *slowed*, precisely, but *changed* in his years away from Melucha.

He checked his chair carefully before he sat, and turned an unenthusiastic gaze to the pile of correspondence. His father still delegated all the interesting, *important* work to his brother Abhinav, while Kalban had the under-clerk's job of writing painstaking replies to people complaining about lost umbrellas. Allegedly this was because Kalban needed to understand the way the city worked before he could be a *real* part of its administration.

He was halfway through the stack before he came to the envelope with his name on it.

There were no other markings on the envelope and no indication of the sender, just a blob of yellow sealing wax holding it shut.

Kalban tugged at the corners, bent it, shook it. When no poisoned needles emerged, he slit it with his paperknife.

A single sheet fell out.

On it was a crude drawing of a snake and one sentence in block capitals.

GO BACK TO MADH BEFORE WE TAKE
MORE DRASTIC MEASURES.

Chapter I

The city of Melucha perched glimmering beside the River Nati, a short distance from the delta whose farmers supplied it with wheat. Unlike distant Madh, whose golden-domed Academy and palace owed their shine as much to sorcery as to gold, Melucha came by its glimmer honestly. It was said that there were more diamonds, rubies, emeralds, sapphires, garnets and opals in that one city-state than in the rest of the Free Lands combined.

The people of Melucha had a taste for fine things.

They also had a taste for dark things. Some maps have warnings, such as 'Here be vampires' or 'Beware of the yaksha militia', at the appropriate places. Any map that included Melucha had to be read with a magnifying glass. Fitting the three hundred and fifty-eight words of the statutory warning into the space between the Nati and the Western Mountains was one of the great challenges of cartography.

At the end of the city nearest the river was the Lotus, as the seat of the Prince Regnant was known—both for the pale pink marble of which it was constructed and for its impenetrability. A road of grey and blue cobbles, laid in whorls that either made the viewer dizzy or brought to mind the petals of a full-blown wild rose, led to the Old Town, a neighbourhood of stately arches and columned porticoes populated by a handful of aristocratic families and the small army of cooks, gardeners, maids, valets, secretaries and assorted staff who kept their homes running.

A covered carriage, its doors emblazoned with the white-and-gold coat of arms of one of Melucha's most prominent clans, was rolling down the thoroughfare to the Lotus's Garden Gate in the early evening.

There it paused. A woman lowered the glass and leaned out to admire the black granite nymphs on either side of the entrance, while the gatekeeper looked up her name on the list of the day's approved visitors. A moment later, he nodded to the driver and pulled the lever that opened the gates. The carriage moved on.

Some people liked to point out that the egalitarian Citizens' Gate, which led to the public lawn and audience hall, was open to all, and one didn't have to wait while one's name was verified against a list. These were, of course, people whose names didn't often feature in the list.

The private section of the garden, accessible through the Garden Gate, was separated from the public area by a low brick wall, constructed more for artistic appeal than to keep out enemies. Enterprising individuals who were novices to the business of conspiracy in Melucha sometimes vaulted over the wall at night in an attempt to infiltrate the palace. They were rescued from the ha-ha in the morning by the duty officer of the Palace Guard.

The carriage drew up at the atrium. The footman who had been sitting beside the driver leapt down to open the door.

Two people emerged. The first was the woman who had leaned out at the gate. She was dressed in deep red silks embroidered with gold and silver thread. The jewels at her wrist and throat could have bought a house in some of the less expensive quarters of the city.

She strode through the atrium with an assurance of belonging in its marble splendour, which her companion, despite his equally fine garments, could not match.

As soon as she entered the main hall, a flute sounded a few notes. They were followed by a voice singing:

With eyes like shining stars above,
Behold the lady fair:
Her raiment is of silken thread,
With jewels gleaming in her hair.

The song broke off but the singer's voice went on. 'Perhaps I should make it *eyne*? Or would that be too old-fashioned? I've been told that I should try to be more contemporary.'

'Really?' said the woman, and if her eyne were too shrewd to be described with perfect accuracy as shining stars above, her voice did have a musical quality. '*That's* the best you can do?'

The court bard, sliding his flute into his scarlet cummerbund, made an extravagant bow. 'The Lady Rati must pardon me. I had only a few hours' notice of your visit, or I would have prepared something more appropriate. It's delightful to see you, my lady. You've been out of favour with our gracious Prince in the past.'

Rati made an impatient noise. 'Stop talking like a bad imitation of an ancient court romance. Nobody's listening. If bribery were such a crime, we'd all be out of favour.'

'I believe the Prince objected not so much to the fact that you bribed his son's tutor to provide information about his activities as to the lack of finesse with which it was accomplished. He thought handing over a pouch of gold in broad daylight showed a distressing level of crudeness for someone seeking to influence a future contender to the throne.'

'He's willing to make peace now.' There was satisfaction in Rati's tone. 'He's offered to restore my seat on the Privy Council. He thinks he's made his point, and he hopes I've had enough time to reflect on the standard of behaviour expected of a Councillor—or so he said in his letter.' She laughed. 'I suppose he means next time I should slide a pigeon's-egg ruby into the tutor's pocket as I pass him in the hall.'

'I wouldn't be too certain of the Prince's favour. The rumour in the palace is that it was Kalban who insisted on having you, much against his father's wishes.'

'Kalban?' There was a sudden thrill of excitement in Rati's voice. 'Is it true, Amar? He's calling himself Kalban now? I thought Avi had made that part of it up; everyone knows he's imaginative.'

'He didn't make this up. It's Kalban. He says he would find it strange to answer to anything else now. He's taken his Tests, you know. He's a Licenced Magician.'

'So I heard. Has his time in Madh improved him?'

'Is that likely?' The court bard smiled. 'Other than attending Privy Council meetings, he's kept to his room. He isn't happy about being back, either. His *other* interests could be indulged with far more freedom in Madh.'

Rati looked as if she had several questions she wanted to ask, but the door at the other end of the hall opened and an attendant entered to announce that the Prince was ready to receive them.

'Is anyone else here tonight?' Rati whispered to Amar as the attendant ushered them into the corridor.

'Only old Kras and his wife.'

To *him* that was clearly unimportant news compared to Kalban's return, but Rati's thrill of excitement turned into something that made her stomach writhe.

'*Kras?* Kras the former Royal Tutor?'

Amar smiled at her discomfiture. 'To be precise, Kras the former Royal Tutor whom you bribed with a pouch of gold, in broad daylight, to listen at doors and tell you what he heard. Quite a reunion, isn't it?'

'The Prince dismissed him after the incident. What's he doing here?'

'Kalban is responsible for Kras's return, too. He's acquired some unusual habits after his stay in Madh.'

There was no time for further inquiry, because the attendant opened the sitting-room door.

The west-facing windows admitted the last of the sunlight. Its golden glow illuminated walls inlaid with sapphire peacocks, brocade curtains and the lithe figure of the Princess Consort.

Princess Persis had been a young sorceress of legendary beauty when she had married the Prince. She was an older sorceress now, but her beauty was undiminished. She was a powerful magician, particularly by the standards of Melucha, where too much supernatural ability was considered vulgar excess.

Beside her, the Prince Regnant, despite the pearls sewn into his relatively simple workday attire, seemed to stand in shadow. One might have written him off as a cipher, one of those handsome but essentially ornamental royal sprigs who exist solely to ensure that their family's genes are passed on.

One would have been wrong. Ornamental he was, and would have been more ornamental had he not insisted on cultivating a goatee that gave a sinister cast to his features. But had his appearance been his only qualification, he wouldn't have lasted as long as he had in a court where two in three rulers died of unnatural causes.

As she moved forward to take Persis's extended hand, Rati's gaze lingered, just for a second, on Abhinav, who stood to one side with his brother. It was a pity that he was the younger son. In every other respect he was the ideal future Prince Regnant. He had inherited his father's aristocratic profile and political acumen, and none of his mother's magical ability. History, in the form of the Purple Revolution, the Ten Days' War and the Wildflower Massacre, had shown that magic couldn't coexist with peace on the throne of Melucha.

Unfortunately, the current Privy Council was composed almost entirely of firstborns who had forced their siblings, when the time came to divide their parents' estates, to content themselves with half an acre of arid land where nothing grew but briars—and that was if they were feeling generous. Leda the Wise had given her brother a cracked earthenware jug and the name of a good potter.

When, on the death or abdication of the sitting Prince Regnant, his successor was chosen from among his heirs, there was no doubt that the Privy Council would make all possible allowances for the claims of primogeniture, and none at all for merit.

As Rati responded to Persis's polite, disinterested questions about the state of her daughter's education (making satisfactory progress), the production on her estates (dismal) and the state of her own health after her recent lying-in (it was iniquitous how much a good midwife could charge), she glanced at the other young man in the room.

Kalban's education in Madh seemed only to have made him less suited to any role in the governance of Melucha. He hadn't been the most promising of children. No amount of coaching and prompting from his parents had been able to conceal the fact that he had middling abilities and a nervous temperament.

However, he had shown some early aptitude for negotiation. Rati remembered a tendency to persuade his tutor that when he assigned an eight-page essay as homework, what he really meant was two pages in large handwriting.

In the hands of a more competent instructor than the dotard Kras, he might have been moulded.

Of course, instead of staying in Melucha to be moulded, he had run away. The Royal Academy at Madh might be renowned through the Free Lands for the quality of its education in Science, Magic and the Arts, but its Political Science courses were dismal.

The Governor of the Southern Provinces of Pür wasn't known for his statesmanship either.

She realized she had spoken the last sentence aloud, in response to a remark from Persis that the Master Sorcerer had sent some very fine rare volumes for their library.

'No,' agreed the Prince, casting a dissatisfied glance at Kalban. 'Political acumen isn't among his talents. His daughter takes after him in that respect. We are, of course, delighted to be of assistance in the matter.'

'Assistance?' Rati asked. 'How are we assisting Madh? Is Kalban going back??' She tried not to sound to hopeful; she hated being discourteous.

'No,' Persis said. 'The Master Sorcerer's daughter is coming here. She'll be taking her Licence Tests next year. I understand from Paras's letter that in every branch of *magical* knowledge her tutors consider her ready for them. But she barely achieved passing marks in Negotiation and Political Science. Her uncle, with an eye to her future role, asked us if she could spend the next two months studying in Melucha.'

'The court of Melucha has the finest scholars of Political Science in the Mortal Realms,' said the Prince, letting his gaze linger on his elder son. 'It's never too late to learn. Just short of sixteen isn't a vast age . . .'

'Political Science can't be taught in two months,' said a soft voice.

Rati suppressed a visible start.

He had been sitting so still, clad in the pearly robe of the philosopher, that he blended in with the marble statues lining the walls. It was Kras, hair and beard as white as his garments, who had spoken from his seat in the corner.

'It can't,' responded Abhinav. 'But according to Kalban, Meenakshi doesn't need to know much. The Governor of Madh gets by with magic.'

'Is it true that he made it rain indoors just to annoy someone who was asking for lower taxes?' Rati asked.

'How uncouth,' said Kras.

'But effective, you must admit,' said Abhinav. 'All that's needed is for her to learn enough to make a respectable showing in her next exam, so that her uncle doesn't have minor fits at the thought of the fate of the city when she rules it. Kalban took pity on poor beleaguered Asamanjas and persuaded Kras to come back for this.'

Kalban compressed his lips.

At Rati's side, Dev spoke for the first time since they'd entered the sitting room. '*You're* going to teach her Political Science? The disgraced former Royal Tutor?'

Rati trod on his foot. He scowled, but fell silent.

'Kras will not be taking on this onerous task alone,' the Prince interjected into the gap. 'Varo was delighted to offer his services as well. Paras's daughter will find her stay in Melucha beneficial.'

'Varo?' said Dev, sliding his foot out of Rati's reach. 'Varo can *teach*? Tonight is full of surprises.'

Varo was Melucha's First Minister. He had been born a commoner. His intelligence and capacity for hard work had carried him up through the ranks of the city's lower officials until he came to the attention of the Prince, who was always on the lookout for talent he could hire, especially since talent hired by him was often removed from the pool of talent available for hire by his enemies.

There was no denying that Varo was a clever statesman. Some people called him brilliant. Rati wasn't one of them.

Varo had, after Kras's unfortunate dismissal, taken over Abhinav's education. It had been Varo's maiden foray into teaching. He couldn't have had an apter pupil. Abhinav had needed little instruction in the arts that counted in Melucha.

But the idea of Varo imparting his instinctive ability to navigate the currents of court to a girl who had barely passed the childish Political Science courses of Madh was absurd. It was like a crocodile trying to teach a rabbit to glide silently through water to its prey: impossible, and rabbits weren't meant to swim in any case. Or to hunt fish.

'He's happy to do his part towards the maintenance of international relations,' said Persis. 'It'll be a new challenge for him.'

'If you have any concerns about his fitness,' said the Prince, 'feel free to address them to him directly. He is expected tonight.'

Into the suddenly tense atmosphere came the sound of Amar clearing his throat and the rustle as he took out his flute from his cummerbund.

To general relief, the announcement of Varo's arrival prevented Amar from beginning a song.

Varo, on entry, bowed to the Prince and Princess. He was dressed in a sensible tunic—no long philosophers' robes for him to trip over—and his beard was trimmed to a reasonable length instead of being allowed to dangle uncombed to his waist as though he hoped to attract homeless weaver birds.

It was a shame he was so loyal to the Prince, thought Rati. She had made several overtures to him over the years. They had all been rebuffed.

'I was surprised to receive your invitation, Your Highness . . . delighted, of course. Your suggestion was . . . interesting.'

'Kalban's playing politics,' Abhinav said.

The look Kalban shot him would have frozen anybody less thick-skinned. Abhinav laughed, with just enough malice to be noticeable without calling down a reproof.

'You managed to instil a basic understanding of politics in my brother,' Kalban said. 'I thought you might be willing to help Meenakshi. I'm sure the Governor will be grateful for any assistance we can render.'

Rati shuddered. Kalban would need some training if he wasn't to disgrace the name of Melucha. If only Abhinav had been born first.

She didn't know why she and Dev had been invited to dinner. Neither of them could be expected to teach this young foreign magician. Rati couldn't add to Varo's sum of knowledge, and as for Dev . . . subtlety wasn't among his strong points. He was a highly-regarded sculptor of the modern school, who had no trouble selling his work so long as Rati arranged for large sums of money to be paid over to the proprietors of the local auction houses. But that was the extent of his skill.

The flute interrupted her thoughts with a few notes from a cheerful song about twelve boys at a feast.

Persis nodded.

'Thank you for the reminder, Amar. I think it's time for dinner.'

Chapter II

Kalban couldn't hold back a groan. Dinners in Melucha were interminable, even when it was just the family. Tonight they also had a decrepit philosopher, a career politician, the proudest aristocrat in Melucha and her husband, who was either a shameless gold-digger or an underappreciated artist, depending on whom you asked. The only person who wasn't participating in the conversation was Kras's wife, Angana, who had barely raised her eyes from her plate.

Entire civilizations might have risen and fallen in the time they'd been sitting at the table.

Kalban couldn't even console himself by cursing the perpetrator. It had been his own doing.

He missed meals in Madh. The food was inferior to what was served in Melucha, which attracted as many excellent cooks as it did renowned artists. There were no sculptures to gaze at in Madh, and no fine dresses except at state dinners, when the officials of the Inter-Realm Liaison Bureau could be expected to do themselves well in the matter of silks and gemstones.

Kalban even, astonishing though it was, missed the very real danger of encountering a rogue yaksha in the Jasmine Garden. It was preferable to stepping on a cobra that someone had dropped out of a second-floor window.

The last dish was brought in—an elaborate confection of spun sugar made to look like the Lotus. No magic would have gone into its making. Before he had left, unnecessary magic had been considered dishonourable in Melucha. And Melucha was the sort of place where rulers and courtiers came and went, helped on the way out by interested parties with enough money to acquire little-known western poisons, but *systems* never changed.

Take dinner, for instance.

Long ago, the rulers of Melucha had had official food tasters, as a necessary precaution against the unpleasant possibilities arising from the fact that poisonous plants were sold in bunches at every street corner. Once the general public had become aware of its rights, its disapproval of the practice had become more and more vocal until people were saying it with large stones thrown through the palace windows.

Alisa the Reformer, famed in history for her generosity and among her descendants for her sturdy common sense, had realized that prudence lay in discontinuing the practice before the people, growing tired of waiting for stones to have an effect, started saying it with battleaxes instead.

Thus had the practice been born of inviting the head of the kitchen to dine with the family every day, sitting lower down the table, served first and from the same platters. The people made no objection to this arrangement. Anyone could see that it was fair. If, as head cook, you had it in for your employers and were unimaginative enough to resort to strychnine in the soup, instead of the numerous other avenues your free access to the palace gave you, you deserved what you got.

The head cook, when Kalban had left Melucha, had been a corpulent, good-tempered woman who ran the kitchen with the precision of a master alchemist. She liked food too much to allow it to be tainted with anything. She was gone now—retired, Abhinav had assured him, not poisoned—and Kalban didn't care for her replacement.

The new autocrat of the kitchen was called Mada. He was too polite, too well dressed and too fond of fiddling with his numerous jewelled bracelets while he pretended not to listen to the conversation. Kalban thought it was silly of him to conceal his eavesdropping when everybody knew he was doing it.

Perhaps Kalban *had* spent too long in Madh.

He poked at his portion of dessert. A spun-sugar balcony broke off with a delicate clink.

The conversation swirled around him. Varo and Kras were arguing about the best way to go about Meenakshi's education. Abhinav, although chiefly occupied with his plate, was interposing the occasional unhelpful remark. His parents were making polite conversation with Dev-the-artist—at least, his father was making polite conversation with Dev-the-artist. His mother was glancing between Kalban and Rati as if she were waiting for a fight to start. And was looking forward to being in the audience.

She was wrong about one thing: Kalban had no intention of starting a fight. He might not know the details of everything that had been happening in court in Melucha while he'd been in Madh. He doubted that people who had been in court in Melucha knew the details of everything that had been happening while he'd been in Madh.

He did know that, when the time came, he could count on Rati to be the leader of the faction trying to persuade, bribe or threaten the Privy Council into confirming Abhinav instead of him. If that failed, she'd be the leader of the faction trying to assassinate him.

As though reading his mind, his mother said, 'I hope you've warned your friend what to expect when she comes here. It would be unfortunate if she got herself murdered in Melucha for lack of simple precautions. I don't know what I would say to her parents.'

'I told Meenakshi,' Kalban said. 'I sent her an annotated edition of *Poisons and How to Recognize Them*. She thought it was funny.'

'Oh, *Kalban*,' said his mother, in the exasperated tone that he *hadn't* missed in Madh, because he'd heard it regularly from Paras, Asamanjas and the Chair of Mathematics at the Academy. It was amazing how many people were in a quandary about whether Kalban was being deliberately dense or just couldn't help it.

Persis shot a quick glance at Rati under lowered lashes. Kalban realized the remark had been intended for her. He really *was* bad at reading cues. But . . . why Rati? A warning? Rati wouldn't go *that* far. It was one thing to put venomous snakes in Kalban's bed. Trying to assassinate a visitor was bad form. Trying to assassinate Meenakshi would be a diplomatic disaster. The Maharaja of Pür might not see eye-to-eye with the Governor of the Southern Provinces on many matters, but he was bound to take exception to harm coming to his daughter in Melucha.

And the severing of diplomatic ties would turn the Privy Council against Kalban, particularly if they thought he should have done something about it–

Oh.

Oh.

Kalban stared at Rati, who returned the gaze with a gentle smile.

'You've warned her that we're not as licentious as the people of Madh, I hope,' she said.

Kalban managed not to cringe. Madh's complete disregard for the corollaries and subsections of the International Magic Licensing Regulations was a byword in the Free Lands.

Every letter he had sent Meenakshi since Asamanjas had suggested her visit to Melucha—and, since Asamanjas had suggested her visit to Melucha, he had written at least once a week—included a detailed description of how much trouble Meenakshi could expect to be in if she so much as conjured a pocket handkerchief outside the palace, and how unlikely it was that the matter would be settled with rolled eyes and comments about students needing to experiment, or how would they *learn*?

'She is aware, of course, of the regulated nature of public magic,' he said.

And, if he had anything to say about it, she would spend most of her time in the Lotus, in the private area, so that when she decided that regulations were for other people, at least it wouldn't be anybody else's business.

'Is it true that the granddaughter of the Maharaja of Pür is to be married next year?' Rati asked, blatantly changing the subject.

'We've had an invitation,' said Kalban's mother.

'I'm surprised the Maharaja has consented.' Rati sipped her wine. 'I was told she had betrothed herself to a *most* unsuitable young man.'

'I believe the intention is to have a swayamvara. The princess is a keen archer. The Maharani hopes that some other suitor might display sufficient skill to supplant the unsuitable youth.'

'It's such a pity that Kalban isn't ten years older. He has other talents that are more important than archery, and it would have been such a suitable match for him. I hear she's beautiful.'

'How would it have been a suitable match?' asked Kalban coldly. 'The Maharaja's granddaughter is second in line to the throne. I would have to leave Melucha and live in Pür if I married her.'

'It would be a terrible loss for us. But when I consider how valuable your services—and your abilities—would have been to the kingdom of Pür, I feel that it would have been right for Melucha to let you go in the interest of the greater good. But since you *are* far too young, we won't be called upon to make the sacrifice.'

'We can't be certain of that,' said Abhinav. 'There'll be many distinguished visitors. Kalban might make new friends.'

Kalban scowled. He hadn't realized Abhinav was paying attention.

'Quite right,' quavered Kras, distracted from the intricacies of pedagogy by the more pressing question of which foreign princess could be persuaded to take Kalban off their hands. 'The High Lord of Vraja has two daughters. The elder is around your age, Kalban. It's too early to think of marriage, but in a few years . . .'

'She has an older brother, though,' said Abhinav.

Kras made a gesture that dismissed the firstborn child of the High Lord of Vraja as inconsequential. 'Vraja is a dangerous country. Anything might happen. The last Maharaja of Pür died there in a hunting accident. It was a tragedy.'

The conversation halted at a signal from Kalban's father. The company rose to repair to the drawing room. Mada followed, escorting Angana, since her husband had resumed his argument with Varo.

As he padded through the carpeted hall, only half listening to Kras's lecture on some obscure point of philosophy that had recently been put forth by a Yaunic scholar, he had that sense of impending doom that was familiar from his stay in Madh—which, since coming to Melucha, he had never felt. Not even on that first morning when he had forgotten to shake his letters out before opening them and had almost been stung by the scorpion that emerged from an otherwise unremarkable scroll.

In Madh, he had learnt that the first thing to do when he had such a feeling was to send Meenakshi a copy of the Inter-Realm Code of Sorcery and have Asamanjas slip another under Paras's study door. Here . . .

Kalban shook himself. He had invited at least two people whose most fervent hope was that he would predecease his brother, and show the good taste to do so before succession became an issue. This wasn't the time for inattention.

All the same, he found it very difficult to focus on the present as they settled into the hard chairs his father thought adequate for the comfort of guests he hoped didn't intend to stay very long. After the carafe of wine was brought, tasted and poured into nine glasses, Abhinav asked, 'You're still an abstainer?'

'I find alcohol has an undesirable effect on my judgement,' Kras said.

It was then that Kalban noticed that a teapot and two cups had been brought up along with the wine.

'You prefer tea?'

'An infusion of the plant known in the Eastern Isles as bitterleaf, along with some other herbs,' said Kras, ever the pedant bent on instruction. 'It's a mixture of my own devising. I have been taking it for years, as you know. Bitterleaf has many medicinal benefits. It is known to improve memory. Perhaps you should have some.'

It was almost like old times, before he'd started hearing whispers, before Madh . . . before everything.

Mada poured the tea into both cups, took one and sipped. He wrinkled his nose. 'It tastes foul.'

Kras took the other cup.

'It is the smell that I find unpleasant,' he said. 'I wish there were some way of changing that. The taste is tolerable, with a generous allowance of honey, but the aroma is difficult to endure.'

'Don't worry,' Abhinav said. 'The wine isn't very good either.'

Persis took a sip of hers. 'It's practically vinegar. Send it back. Ask for a new cask.'

Mada went to instruct and, from his expression, harangue whichever member of the kitchen staff had been responsible for the wine.

Conversation flagged. Dev got to his feet and and began examining the paintings on the far wall. He made several pointed remarks about brushstrokes in Persis's direction until, unable to ignore him, she went to listen to his hints about being hired for a portrait. Rati strolled to the window.

Kalban rose as well. The air was stifling. He wished he could have a walk–on one of the balconies, since the garden at night was full of traps for the unwary. Perhaps he could go out after everyone had left.

He wasn't the only one who felt the need for a walk. Other than Kras and Angana, the party started to wander about the room, commenting on books, art and the view. New wine appeared, was tasted, poured and handed around, but the damage had been done. Nobody was inclined to linger.

Assailed by a sudden suspicion, Kalban turned to stare in his father's direction. From the taste, the cask of wine had been broached at least a week ago, and probably stored under direct sunlight. That didn't happen by *accident*.

Kras was the first, barely fifteen minutes after he'd finished his tea, to plead tiredness and ask to retire for the night. Since he was staying in the palace, as part of Kalban's plan to allow Meenakshi's education to be superintended without the drama that would result from her going into the city, he retired to his room. A carriage was called for Angana, who, despite Kalban's mother's invitation to stay at least for this night, was returning home.

This time Kalban correctly interpreted his mother's glance, and walked with Angana into the entrance hall.

'You needn't trouble yourself,' she said. 'I know my way.'

'You and your husband lived here for several years—and more recently than I did,' Kalban agreed, conscious again of his long absence. 'I hope you weren't *too* bored this evening.'

With a clatter of hooves, a closed carriage drew up to the stairs.

'I had a lovely time. It was very kind of your parents to invite me,' Angana said with prim correctness as Kalban helped her in. He waited long enough to see the Garden Gate open on its soundless hinges before he returned to the library.

The party broke up soon afterwards. Feeling vaguely dissatisfied, Kalban took his walk and went to bed.

It was almost dawn when he was awoken from disturbed dreams in which flocks of griffons descended on Melucha and turned into giant scorpions. After a moment's disorientation, he realized someone was banging on his door.

'Coming,' he called.

Going through the ritual of shaking out his slippers and scanning the floor for tripwires as quickly as possible, he went to the door.

Abhinav was outside.

'Kras is dead,' he said without ceremony.

'*What?*'

'Could I have been any clearer? Kras. Is. Dead.'

'Dead? *How?* He . . . he wasn't *that* old.'

Abhinav looked at him like he had been found throwing stones at a beehive.

'Mother thinks it's poison.'

'Kras has been *poisoned*? But it's been hours since dinner.'

'Are you going to repeat everything I say?' Abhinav said testily. 'We don't know exactly when it happened. His wife wasn't staying here. He was alone in his room. He'd asked one of the attendants to wake him up for those foul early-morning exercises . . .'

'Thank all the gods I'm done with those,' Kalban muttered, and then flushed.

Abhinav seemed not to notice anything untoward in his remark. 'Exactly,' he said. 'Anyway, the man went in and found him unresponsive. Since there were no signs of violence and Kras was clearly past help, he informed the safety team.'

'Is there anything left of last night's dinner to analyse?'

'I doubt it. The physician says it was either hemlock or belladonna—he'll know more once he's completed his examination.'

'How do you know all this?'

'I didn't sleep very well last night. Maybe it was too much of that sugar thing. The noise woke me up. The guards are questioning Mada now.'

'Is *he* . . .'

'He's fine. And so are the rest of us. That makes it very unlikely, doesn't it, that the poison was in last night's dinner? Maybe Kras had a secret nightcap—or a secret visitor.'

Chapter III

'Letter from Kalban,' Asamanjas announced at the lunch table.

His niece Meenakshi, her mind on a new alchemical method she was testing, the likelihood of being able to finish her experiment before she had to go to Melucha, and the likelihood of her uncle's finding and dismantling her apparatus in her absence, didn't respond. His brother Paras, his mind on a new alchemical method he was testing and the likelihood of being able to finish his experiment before Asamanjas found out and nagged him about regulations and forms and protocol, didn't respond.

'*Letter from Kalban*,' Asamanjas said again, in a tone that both his brother and his niece recognized as requiring instant attention.

They gave it.

'Does he have anything interesting to say?' Meenakshi asked.

'Apparently,' said Asamanjas, 'there's been a murder.'

Paras shrugged. 'Oh, that's all? I thought something *bad* had happened. It's Melucha. Murder is what they do.'

Meenakshi nodded her agreement. Based on the reading list Kalban had sent her, with the promise of an exam as soon as she set foot in Melucha, you couldn't exist for five minutes without someone attempting to poison you or push you out of a high window or have you eaten by a panther.

'I agree,' said Asamanjas. 'Kalban knows that too. He thinks it's a matter of concern because the victim was one of the tutors who had been selected for Meenakshi.'

'I'll put off my trip while they find another, shall I?' Meenakshi suggested. 'Then I'll have time to finish—'

'Nice try. You're going. Unless you *want* to wait another year to start your Fellowship studies because you can't come up to scratch in Negotiation.'

'The professors won't insist that I wait,' Meenakshi pointed out. 'I won't need Negotiation to study Alchemy.'

'I daresay not, but you *will* need Negotiation when you are in charge of the governance of this city and I intend to see that your skills are less egregious than your father's. Your mother agrees. She wasn't happy about that last exam.'

'You told *Mother*?'

'Your father told her.'

Meenakshi turned to Paras in outrage. 'We had an agreement! There's no need to worry her with trivial matters when she's doing much more important work—'

'Your mother would consider your education important,' said Paras, but without any real conviction. 'Besides, she would have been angry if she'd found out later and I hadn't told her.'

'The point is,' said Asamanjas, 'that, if nothing else, the experience of a foreign court will be beneficial. You're going.'

Meenakshi knew better than to argue. Ever since Kalban had left, her uncle's efforts in the cause of her education had doubled. It was as though he'd entertained a hope that Kalban would decide to stay and help her, unlikely as it had been that the court of Melucha would countenance such a thing for a minute. Even if it was true that, as Kalban said, most of the court wanted his brother in charge instead of him, they didn't want Kalban away in Madh fomenting rebellion. They wanted him in Melucha where they could keep an eye on him and, if necessary, make good use of panthers.

'I'm sure Kalban can find a replacement,' Paras said. 'If the court of Melucha can't produce good teachers of the Political Sciences . . .'

'Oh, yes, that's not the main concern. Other than his very natural sorrow at an unexpected death–'

'He's not sorry at all, is he?' asked Meenakshi.

'I can't tell from his letter,' Asamanjas admitted. 'But since he spent several years in Madh and it's only been four months since he returned to the land of barbaric customs–'

'You said I wasn't allowed to call it that!' Paras said indignantly.

'I said you weren't allowed to call it that in the public speech you made at Kalban's farewell dinner. We're in private now. In any case, we'll give Kalban the benefit of the doubt and assume he feels the appropriate amount of grief. The real problem, as always, has been caused by Inter-Realm meddling.'

That caught both Paras's and Meenakshi's interest, as he had known it would.

'It appears,' Asamanjas went on, at leisure now that he was certain of his audience, 'that a Celestial Dancer–' He paused to consult Kalban's letter. 'Chitralekha. He says you know her, Meenakshi. Wasn't she the one who caused that trouble with the Thoughtform?'

'Chitralekha didn't *cause* it,' Meenakshi said. 'She was the one who was here, yes.'

'My apologies. She *has* caused trouble now. I understand that Kalban and Persis are both on the Dancers' watch list–particularly Persis, who does have something of an unfortunate history–'

'I know she used to turn people into pigs,' Meenakshi said, unimpressed. 'Kalban already told me animal transformation spells aren't allowed in Melucha, even on provocation, and when they say not allowed they mean *not allowed* and not *please read this pamphlet about the Code of Sorcery.*'

'It's a good thing that Kalban is in Melucha to keep an eye on you,' muttered Asamanjas. 'Be that as it may, since a murder has occurred in the vicinity of two of the people on their list–in their very home, I understand–the Dancers thought it merited investigation.'

'The Dancers track non-magical crimes now?' Meenakshi asked. 'Why don't they keep turning up in Madh? There must be at least a dozen people on their list here.'

'More than a dozen, but they use their judgement,' Asamanjas said. 'Madh monitors magical activity closely and there's enough Inter-Realm traffic that they needn't worry about non-magical crimes. Which, incidentally, I didn't say this was. Did Kalban tell you anything about it?'

'No, but if it *were* a magical crime they wouldn't need to *investigate*, would they? They could trace the residues.'

'They might not have the capacity. Since there are far fewer practitioners in Melucha, magic is so highly regulated that those who have the ability and want to hone it prefer to leave, if they can. Which brings me to my point. Since the Celestial Dancers are investigating it as a potential abuse of power, far stricter regulations are in effect in Melucha until the investigation is complete.'

'How much stricter can they *be*? Unlicensed public magic is already banned.'

'Earlier a violation would get you fined. Now you might be deported, and that would be *you* getting off lightly to avoid an international incident. There's also something about public assembly of practitioners that I won't attempt to explain to you. Since this has the potential to cause an awkward situation all round, Kalban thinks you should stay within the boundaries of the palace until the matter is resolved. If you're not in public, there's no possibility of a violation.'

Meenakshi shrugged. 'Kalban said they have a decent library.'

Asamanjas, who had been expecting more of a fight, found himself, for once, thanking all of creation that his niece had little interest in interaction with other human beings.

Two days later, accompanied by her secretary Gopali, Meenakshi made her way to the Portals Hall. For some reason fathomable only to its original planners, the hall had been built four miles outside the city limits. It was a large, airy building in the Yaunic style, with a colonnaded façade through which, although it was early, a line of people snaked back and forth.

'Registering their luggage,' Gopali said, seeing Meenakshi's look. 'It'll be searched at their destination. Madh permits the possession of a number of dangerous magical substances, for research and teaching at the Academy. Other cities don't allow them. Don't worry. Our things have been sent ahead, so we don't have to stand in that line.'

Meenakshi hadn't been to the Portals Hall since she had accompanied her parents and uncle on their last visit to the Maharaja, two years ago now. Several changes had taken place since then. The Inter-Realm Border Crossing was now sectioned off, but through an open door she caught a glimpse of a yaksha arguing with a bored-looking official.

She would have stayed to see what was happening, but Gopali hustled her on. There were several lines, mercifully short ones. Then she was given a form that appeared to be an aspiring three-volume novel and demanded so much information about her antecedents and personal history that Meenakshi, frequently at a loss, had to consult Gopali.

Gopali, having dealt with her own form with brisk efficiency, took over Meenakshi's.

'You're Category 4,' she said. 'Unlicenced underage practitioner registered as a student. Now go to the next page and fill subsection a. Put down *no* for everything. Yes, even the one about whether you've ever contravened the spirit of the Alchemical Beasts (Creation) Accord. The Arcane Zoology Authorization Desk keeps sending you pamphlets, but you've never formally been charged. Good, now on to subsection b . . .'

Thanks to Gopali, five minutes later they were entering the large room where the portals were. A clerk took their forms, stamped them, and demanded in a tone of accusation, 'Melucha? Taking the magical curriculum at the Academy?' On receiving an affirmative answer to both questions, he thrust a form at Meenakshi. 'You need to sign a release and liability waiver. There's Section 39 in Melucha now.'

Presuming that Section 39 involved whatever it was about public assembly that her uncle hadn't wanted to explain, Meenakshi signed the form. Then he was waving them through to the line leading to the portal marked *Melucha*.

A few minutes later, she was stepping out of the portal at the other end. Gopali, right behind her, steered her to the immigration desk. Another three forms and an unpleasant interview with an immigration official bent on explaining the provisions and subsections of Section 39, and they were walking out of the hall.

Meenakshi noticed that the Inter-Ream Border Crossing section in Melucha was much smaller than the one in Madh–it wasn't even a separate room, just a single portal roped off from the main hall. Nobody was going through in either direction.

Perhaps Melucha was more different than she'd thought.

As they stepped out of the building, they were seized upon by a miniature whirlwind. It took a moment for Meenakshi to recognize Chitralekha.

'What are you doing here?'

'Kalban was going to come,' Chitralekha said. 'He wanted to get in right away and lecture you about all the laws you're not supposed to break–'

'I've already heard about Section 39–'

'That's just one of them. There are more. I won't ask you to be grateful to me for sparing you that, because you'll have to listen to it very soon. I wanted to speak to you alone first.

Hello—Gopali, isn't it?' Chitralekha added to Gopali. 'Come along. The carriage is waiting.'

'Kalban sent a carriage?'

'You're not allowed to ride or walk in Melucha unless you're a penniless artist. I'm told it clutters up the landscape. Here we are.'

It was a large carriage with four matched horses. Emblazoned in navy blue on the doors was what Meenakshi recognized as the coat of arms of Melucha.

'They do themselves well in this city,' she said, when she clambered in and saw the velvet-covered cushioned seats, also blue.

'You haven't seen anything yet.'

As the carriage began to move down the cobbled road, Chitralekha said, 'I suppose you knew I was here.'

'Kalban told my uncle. Is it something that needs to involve the Inter-Realm? From everything he's said, murder in Melucha is like . . . like . . .'

'Like unauthorized Alchemy in Madh?' asked Chitralekha with a grin. 'True. And—I don't know if you know the details—the man wasn't killed by magic anyway.'

'I knew he couldn't have been. That would have brought down more than just you.'

'Rambha would have come in person, with the heavy weaponry. Kras was poisoned. Hemlock. Of course, that doesn't mean the person who did it doesn't have magical ability. The Captain of the Palace Guard has turned in a finding of murder by a party unknown. The Prince has accepted it. *We* don't. Their investigation was perfunctory. They questioned everyone who was at dinner that day and, when nobody confessed to the crime, left it at that. But two powerful magic users were in the same building, both with sufficient political influence to affect the outcome of a local investigation.'

'Don't you spend a lot of time investigating in Melucha?'

'Less than you'd think. You're judging by Madh. Its population has a far higher proportion of magic users, because of the Academy . . . and the culture. In most other cities you could meet a hundred people and maybe two or three will be able to use magic with any sort of proficiency. Fewer would be on our watch list. Persis is a foreigner, remember?'

'Kalban's *mother* murdered the tutor?'

'Look at that. You read up. Yes, he's the tutor, or to be specific the *former* tutor, and please don't say I accused the Princess of murder. I *don't* know who killed him. But—all right, I'll tell you,' she said, dropping her voice. 'You *can't* repeat this to anyone.'

'Tell anyone what?'

'The initial report from the Surveillance and Reconaissance Division—that's mainly Sprites—has Kalban as the probable culprit.'

'Kalban wouldn't have,' Meenakshi protested. 'It must be a violation of at least a dozen different statutes and international treaties.'

'Don't be too sure of that,' Chitralekha said grimly. 'It's like Madh and Alchemy. Melucha has a tendency to bring out any murderous impulses people are suppressing.'

'Kalban –'

'I'm not saying he did it. The report is just an opinion, not proof. Nor is it an accusation. He wouldn't have been my first pick, with so many other candidates. But we *must* be certain. That's why I'm here.'

CHAPTER IV

Rati walked into Dev's workroom as though she owned it; in fact, she did.

'What is it?' he asked, pausing with his chisel raised. 'I can't have distractions now. I'm getting this piece ready for the exhibition at the Grand Gallery next month.'

'What are you making?'

'A reflection on the fragility of existence.' With a put-upon sigh, Dev laid the chisel on the top rung of the stepladder and descended. 'Is it something important?'

Rati studied the nascent sculpture with pursed lips. It was a fine block of marble; even unpolished it looked faintly luminescent. It was a pity Dev liked to focus on the ugliness of things. She'd have to hand out a few ruby bracelets to the Council of Art. No matter. She had always known that supporting Dev's artistic career would be an expensive proposition.

She glanced at the note in her hand.

'I've just had word from the palace. The girl's arrived.'

'You're arranging for hemlock in *her* soup?'

'Don't be ridiculous,' said Rati. 'I don't murder *children*. I'll need you to take a message for me—two messages.'

'I'm busy,' Dev said.

'This is important. I can't go myself. I can't trust it to a paid courier. The agent will meet you at the usual place . . . It won't take you more than half an hour if you take the carriage. There's also a package.'

Dev looked disgruntled, but he took off his smock and followed her from the room.

Meenakshi took to Persis as soon as she met her. The twinkle in her eye and something in the way she shook Meenakshi's hand and hoped she'd have enjoyable stay indicated that she, like Meenakshi's father, took a sensible view of the applicability of the Inter-Realm Code of Sorcery. Perhaps the fact that they had been at the Academy together had something to do with that.

About Abhinav she had mixed opinions. From the descriptions Kalban had given her over the years, and the bits of his letters he'd read out, she had been prepared to find a sinister schemer plotting to murder his father and brother and seize the throne. Abhinav welcomed her to Melucha with perfect indifference, but he didn't seem like a parricide-in-waiting.

What surprised her most was the change in Kalban. He had always had a tendency to anxiety, but now he looked like all the worries of the world had come down on his head. His manner managed to cast a pall of gloom even over the sunlit rooms of the Lotus.

It was several hours before she could speak to him alone. The first thing he said was, 'Your lessons with Varo will begin tomorrow.' The second thing was, 'Please don't turn him into anything.'

'I've never turned any of my tutors into anything!'

'And don't leave the palace grounds.'

'I already know about Section 39—'

'It's not that. Well, it *is* that, but we could try to sort it out by pointing out that you're a foreigner who didn't know better. I don't want to try explaining myself to the Master Sorcerer if you get murdered, much less to your uncle.'

'While we're on the subject of murder, don't we have more important things to discuss than regulations?'

'If you're referring to the unfortunate incident with Kras—'

'After all the lecturing you've done, *you* didn't notice him being poisoned right under your nose.'

'It was the tea,' Kalban said. 'It must have been.'

'The tea was poisoned? Isn't it usually soup?'

'Hemlock isn't an easy poison to mask. It has a distinctive smell and taste. We had a very light soup that evening. In the unlikely event that none of the rest of us had smelt it, Kras would have known with the first sip. But the tea . . . he drank a herbal concoction for his health—he'd been taking it for years. Bitter and strong-smelling.'

'You know Chitralekha thinks you did it, don't you?'

'I know. She's pretending she's here as a *precaution*. She's not very good at prevaricating. The Sprites have a point about that. Celestial Dancers tend to be open about what they're thinking. Chitralekha believes it's an attempt to get myself banished so I can go back to Madh.'

'That's stupid,' Meenakshi said.

'Thank you.'

'If you were going to get yourself banished, what point would there be in pretending you didn't do it? You would have planted a lot of clues pointing in your direction.'

Kalban sighed. 'Of *course*, that's the stupid part.'

'Although . . .' Meenakshi said as though giving the matter serious thought for the first time, 'if you wanted to get away, couldn't you leave? You're of age. You wouldn't have to sneak off on a stolen boat this time.'

'I suppose not. But if I left again, of my own volition, I would burn all my bridges in Melucha—or whatever's left of them. If you think the court disapproves of magic, you've not heard my father hold forth on the subject of people who run away. There'd be no coming back except as a black sheep to be relegated to a minor post in the government, at my father's pleasure—or more probably my brother's.'

'Wouldn't murdering your old tutor burn your bridges?'

'Not that much. At worst I'd be banished. It's not unknown for an exiled contender for the throne to return at the head of an army.'

'Who did it, then?'

'I wish I knew.' Kalban shrugged. 'Chitralekha's coming soon—that'll be her now,' he added, as a sharp rap sounded at the door.

'Right,' Chitralekha said, shutting the door behind her. 'I'm here. I've already explained some things to Meenakshi. Kalban's agreed to help me–'

'I was blackmailed into helping you,' Kalban corrected. 'You said you put me on the high alert list and the only way to get myself off it was to prove I didn't murder Kras.'

'If you want to get *technical* . . .'

'What happens if you get put on the high alert list?' Meenakshi asked.

'We keep popping down whenever we detect a spike in his magical activity–'

'And give everyone in Melucha the impression that I'm one broken beaker away from turning into a mad alchemist and destroying the city!'

Unperturbed, Chitralekha produced a sheet of paper. 'I've got a plan of action. Whatever the medium of the poison was–I'm inclined to think that Kalban was right and it was the tea–it must have been done by someone *at* dinner, not before it.'

'That makes sense,' agreed Kalban. 'The head of the kitchen had a normal portion of everything, and he's shown no ill effects. Nor has anyone else.'

'There were ten people at dinner that day. Any of them could have done it–yes, even Kras himself,' she said, in response to Meenakshi's expression. 'We can't eliminate the possibility of suicide.'

'Why would Kras kill himself?'

'That's what we need to find out . . . So, ten people. We need to speak to them all. Except Kras, of course. We'll have to divide them between the two of us, because Kalban is a suspect himself–'

'I didn't kill Kras,' Kalban said, though he sounded more exasperated than offended. 'And whether I'm a suspect or not, do you think Meenakshi is fit to go and interview people in a matter of such delicacy? Are you looking for ways to be demoted? I can suggest some that are far less trouble.'

'Go and interview people? Do I look like the Captain of the City Guard? We don't *interview* people in the Inter-Realm. Meenakshi's going to talk to them. Just *talk*. Or isn't that allowed in Melucha either?'

'I know I'm going to regret this, but . . . fine. If she leaves the palace, I'm going with her.'

'Don't blame me if Rambha thinks your presence makes the evidence inadmissible. Now before we do anything else, we'll start with *you*.' She turned to Meenakshi. 'Lesson one: we're starting with Kalban because, if he's not the murderer, he's likely to tell us the truth. Everyone else has something to hide, so don't believe anybody without corroboration.'

'This is a total waste of time,' Meenakshi muttered. 'Look, the solution is simple. Chitralekha goes and interviews everyone, and we stay here and Scry them. If they're guilty, they'll give themselves away once she's gone by showing some obvious sign of relief.'

'Which you would never recognize,' Kalban pointed out.

'Doesn't matter. You will.'

'That's not a bad idea,' Chitralekha began.

'Don't even think about it,' said Kalban. 'It's completely illegal.'

'There's another thing,' Meenakshi suggested. 'Scrying people in the present is a violation of their privacy—even if they're murderers.'

'Only one of them is a murderer.'

'This time. Are you telling me none of them has had enemies bumped off before?'

'All right, they're all *probably* murderers, but they're still entitled to privacy.'

'Father and I were thinking that some modifications to the spell might work to Scry into the past–'

'No.'

'We won't look at anything else,' Meenakshi assured him. 'No prying. We can see who put the poison in Kras's food–look, all we need is to prove that it wasn't you or your mother, so Chitralekha can go home.'

'She's right,' Chitralekha said. 'I'm not here to investigate non-magicians or take part in mortal squabbles–'

'Are you certain you can Scry the past?' Kalban asked Meenakshi, in the tone of one who already knew the answer. '*Safely?*'

'I've never tried it–'

'So it's possible you won't succeed and you'll rip the fabric of time instead?'

'I'll be careful. You have to take *some* risks when you're experimenting with new forms of magic–'

'This is not a risk we need to take. Not in Melucha. We can't reproduce test conditions, we don't have the equipment or the laboratories, *or* people qualified to help when it goes wrong. We're going to solve this the old-fashioned way.'

'Never mind,' Chitralekha said. 'We can do this without Scrying. Let's get started or we'll never get done. Kalban, what do you remember? Start at the beginning.'

'You mean you want to know the order in which people arrived?'

'Start with dinner.'

'We were in our usual places at the table. Rati and Dev after Abhinav, and Varo and Kras next to me. And Kras's wife, of course, Angana; she was so quiet that nobody noticed she was there. Maybe it's the effect of having lived with Kras all her life. He talks—*talked*—enough for eight normal people.' He caught Chitralekha's eye and grinned. 'I won't ramble. The court bard was opposite her and Mada—the head cook—at the foot of the table.'

'Did everyone eat the same dinner?'

'I think everybody had every course, but I can't be sure. There was nothing at dinner that only Kras ate. I would have noticed that.'

'Mada tasted everything?'

'Yes.'

'Why are we so sure the hemlock was in the tea?' Meenakshi asked. 'Mada tasted the tea too, and if someone added hemlock to Kras's portion, why couldn't it have been to his portion of something else?'

'Nobody left their seats during dinner.'

'Was anyone sitting close enough to Kras?'

'His wife was on one side, Varo on the other. But there was space between them; they couldn't have done it unseen.'

'We'll accept that for now,' Chitralekha said. 'What happened then?'

'We were lingering over the sweet. Talking. It wasn't anything very important. Mother was trying to warn Rati not to make trouble while Meenakshi's here. I don't know if she took the hint.'

'Is Rati planning to make trouble?'

'Underestimating her would be dangerous.'

'We'll talk to her. Move on.'

'We went into the library. The attendant brought in the wine. He poured it and handed it round to everyone except Kras—Mada had a glass first. It wasn't very good; we had to send for more. I think my father arranged that, to disrupt the atmosphere so Rati and Dev would leave.'

'Never mind the wine. That's the one thing we can be sure wasn't responsible for Kras's death.'

'The tea, then. Kras imbibed a foul concoction he claimed was good for his liver and improved his memory. I'm sure it was nonsense, but he had a tendency to believe every charlatan who hung a few jade amulets outside his shop window.'

'He made you drink something revolting when you were a child, didn't he?' asked Chitralekha, very carefully not smiling.

'The same tea. It tasted like something scraped off the bottom of his shoe and boiled in ditchwater.'

'Did he bring it with him?'

'I suppose so. Guests generally do—oh, not tea. If people have tisanes prescribed by physicians, they hand them to the attendant who lets them in. He sees that it's steeped and presented to them at the appropriate time.'

'All right, so Kras, and possibly his wife or someone else in his house, handled the tea, until it was given to the attendant who met them on their arrival. The attendant would take it to the kitchen?'

'There's always a pot of water on boil. When we were children, we snuck in one festival day to get some sweets, and Abhinav almost upset it over himself.' Kalban grinned in fond reminiscence. 'Father was furious. He said it was enough work keeping assassins out of the place, there was no need for us to go doing their job for them.'

'Why doesn't he like Abhinav?' Meenakshi whispered to Chitralekha. 'He didn't seem that bad.'

'Rival claimants to the throne never like each other much. Who drank first? Mada?'

'He had a few sips. Nobody can drink that foul thing quickly. Kras didn't wait for him to finish the cup. It would have gone cold. And *now* we get to the important part,' Kalban went on. 'Mada's tea wasn't poisoned, because he *did* finish the cup, although slowly, and he's still alive. Someone must have added the hemlock to Kras's cup.'

'Did anyone get up and walk around?'

'We all did. Everyone—except Kras, of course—had had a bit of wine. Dev was trying to get Mother to commission a portrait. She never will; he's hopeless. He painted a pair of swans for a festival exhibition when I was a child and nobody could tell what they were. Father thought it was a volcano and Dev was so offended he withdrew his application to paint the throne room mural . . . He took Mother round and talked about brushstrokes and colour mixing. Varo and Kras were discussing Meenakshi's study schedule—you have your first lesson with him in the morning, by the way.'

'Excellent,' said Chitralekha, ignoring Meenakshi's alarm. 'You can start by talking to him.'

'Abhinav was pacing,' Kalban continued. 'He was bored. So was I, but I didn't prowl like a caged tiger. Father stayed seated most of the time, but he got up to speak to Kras's wife. He kept trying to get Abhinav to do it but he wouldn't take the hint. Who's left?'

'Amar,' said Meenakshi.

'Yes, Amar. He was walking around singing songs about the moonlight. Nobody listened. Nobody ever does; he can carry a tune, but his songs are dull.'

'What did you do?' asked Chitralekha.

Kalban shrugged. 'Nothing. I got up and went to the window once, to see if the moonlight was that nice. I've seen better.'

'Is there anyone you can say definitely didn't go near Kras's cup?'

Kalban thought for a moment and shook his head. 'Anyone might have done it. We all passed him at one time or another. Of course, Varo had the best opportunity . . .'

'Then *and* at dinner,' said Meenakshi.

'If anything, I'd say that puts Varo right out of it. If you're going to put hemlock in a man's tea, you don't sit beside him all evening and make yourself a prime suspect. Varo didn't rise to his present position by being a fool.'

Chapter V

Meenakshi was used to occasionally finding Gopali or her other secretary, Saha, in the room when she woke. They took it upon themselves to clear her bedroom and study of any incriminating evidence when they expected a surprise inspection from the Arcane Zoology Authorization Desk. Meenakshi thought it was an excess of caution to take away all her notes and research, including her Mathematics homework and History essay, but since it reappeared intact after the inspectors left, it wasn't worth making a fuss.

There was, however, no Arcane Zoology Authorization Desk in Melucha, and Meenakshi had barely had time to look at a book since her arrival. She couldn't imagine why Gopali was on her hands and knees peering under the bookshelf.

'Do you want something?' she ventured, sitting up in bed.

'Wait,' Gopali ordered, getting to her feet. She was holding something in a cloth. 'Shake out your slippers before you put them on, and I haven't yet checked your clothes.'

Meenakshi groaned and stared up at the painted ceiling, across which a rage of maidens frolicked with a bevy of swans. She could have sworn they were laughing at her. 'Has Kalban got to you, too?'

'There was a venomous spider next to my mirror when I went to bed,' Gopali said. Meenakshi noticed the bundle in her hand wriggling. 'In a place where people breed animals to be murder weapons and don't have the sense to seal the enclosures shut with magic, I don't need Kalban to tell me to be careful.'

With a stifled sigh Meenakshi shook out her slippers, got out of bed and only made a face when Gopali pointed out that the needles in the case on the chest-of-drawers had a suspicious green glint. If people were waiting for her to embroider handkerchiefs before they poisoned her, she had nothing to worry about.

'Do I have to go down to breakfast?' she asked.

'No. The family gathers for lunch and dinner. For breakfast they'll send a tray up. Kalban's coming, though. He wants to brief you on the protocol.'

'Not another lecture on Section 39,' muttered Meenakshi.

Rati looked at the single sheet of paper that had been delivered first thing that morning.

She had known that her initial briefing about the Master Sorcerer's daughter would be, well, *brief*, but if her sources in the palace thought she was going to reward them for half a page of transcribed dinner-time chatter and a drawing that might represent *anyone*, she had obviously been too generous with their payments in the past.

'There must be *something* I can do about it,' she muttered.

She considered finding Dev, but rejected the idea almost at once. Dev helped her out with an occasional delivery because he felt he had to, but there was no point expecting him to discuss the situation with her. He wasn't *really* interested in the future of Melucha. He wasn't interested much in any future, other than his own as an artist. Unlike Rati, he hadn't been raised to believe that it was a sort of collective responsibility to ensure that the person who held the throne of Melucha was the fittest one for it.

She was certain that, in the present case, the person fittest for the throne was Abhinav. Rati, who had several older siblings, didn't subscribe to the general belief that the firstborn had the highest claim—especially not when the firstborn was a sorcerer.

Something would have to be done about Kalban. A pity he hadn't stayed in Madh.

The girl was a complication. She had hoped that, after Kras's death, her uncle would decide against sending her to Melucha. There was the danger that the Privy Council, already sympathetic to the rights of the eldest child, would note how useful it was that Persis had been at school with the Master Sorcerer, and would take Kalban's friendship with his daughter as a point in his favour.

But if there was one thing the Privy Council believed in more strongly than primogeniture, it was that magic was dangerous. Rati had to use that belief. The girl's magical ability—while very important for *her* future role in Madh—was just the thing to spread alarm and despondency among the aristocratic class of Melucha.

Before Rati could decide on a course of action, a bell on one side of the room chimed. She didn't need to look at it—she knew each bell and its tone, and that one was for the gate. She hurried to the balcony, to see an exceptionally beautiful woman dressed in the style of a classical painting mount the steps to the front door.

So there *was* a Dancer—and she was *here*. That meant she wanted something from Rati.

Rati smiled and went downstairs.

As it happened, Meenakshi wasn't subjected to another lecture on Section 39. It was far worse. It was a speech, lasting several minutes and involving a series of diagrams, on why she couldn't trust Varo.

'But,' she said, when at last she could get a word in, with Kalban's last complex drawing dissipating into smoke, 'why would Varo care whether I have a good working relationship with Clever Raman? It's got nothing to do with him.'

'He'll be passing information on to someone on the Privy Council—I don't know who it is yet, but he's an informer. He *must* be.'

'Why didn't you get me a tutor you could trust?'

Kalban's expression of patient suffering was, at least, familiar. 'Haven't you been listening to me? We don't trust *anyone*.'

'You mean Chitralekha,' said Meenakshi, who had enough experience of Kalban by now to understand his veiled hints. 'Don't you?'

'She's hiding something. It's too perfect . . . How did she know to come here? I didn't kill Kras, and if Mother did, it was *hemlock*, not magic. At most, someone used magic to get the hemlock into Kras's cup without going near him. That isn't enough to cause a spike. I refuse to believe they track all Mortal births and deaths. How did she know that Kras died in the Lotus and it was murder?'

'Chitralekha's hiding something. I'll keep that in mind.'

'Good. Come, I'll show you the way to your lesson. Varo won't be pleased if you're late.'

'There's no school here, is there?' said Meenakshi, gathering her books and following Kalban out of the room. 'Does everyone have private tutors?'

Kalban's shoulders twitched uncomfortably.

'There *are* schools . . . they're just . . . limited. They're a relatively new concept. The earlier rulers of Melucha didn't believe in education for the masses. It's easier to control people if they're illiterate and superstitious. The Wildflower Massacre changed that. There's a school in every neighbourhood now, but they're not . . . they're not the Academy. People learn how to read and write and do enough arithmetic to add up their day's takings and know if someone's short-changing them . . . but not so much that moneylenders can't still run them into debt.'

'What do they do if they want to learn more?'

'There are private tutors. That can be expensive. If they can manage it, they go to Madh. The Royal Academy isn't cheap, but there are plenty of scholarships available.'

'Not everyone can manage a scholarship.'

'That's true, but if someone wants to learn, *really* wants to learn, the Board of Trustees finds a way. I don't think anyone's ever been prevented from attending the Academy by lack of money.'

Kalban paused at a door carved with . . . Meenakshi squinted.

'Is that a bear?'

'It's an elephant. Dev's work. I told you.'

Meenakshi raised her hand to knock, but Kalban caught her arm and pulled her back. 'I've not had much of a chance to talk to you privately. Listen to me. You have to be careful.'

'You've not had much of a chance?' Meenakshi said incredulously. 'Do you have any idea how eloquent you were on the subject of not trusting Varo?'

'Anyone could have been listening outside the window. I'm not just talking about who might have killed Kras. There aren't magical traps or unauthorized yakshas in the palace, but if a banded krait bites you, you'll be just as dead.'

'Why are you so nervous?'

'I got so used to relying on magic in Madh that I forgot how to look and listen for things. Like an unexpected snake in a dark room. And *you* never knew to be wary of non-magical traps. Watch where you step. Watch what you touch. Don't trust *anyone*.' He knocked, and opened the door without waiting for an answer. 'Meenakshi's here.'

'Thank you,' said the man sitting at the largest of the room's several tables. 'We'll get to know each other.'

With a final whispered admonition not to do anything alarming, Kalban left Meenakshi with Varo.

Meenakshi studied her new tutor with considerable curiosity. Kalban had, at one time or another, told her a great deal about Kras, who had been his own tutor as a child. She had never heard Varo's name until being informed that he was going to give her lessons in Political Science.

She wasn't sure what she'd expected, but she was surprised by the normalcy of the man who got to his feet and came to greet her with hands outstretched. He took her unresisting fingers in a firm clasp, lasting just long enough for Meenakshi to notice that his hands were cool and dry. Then he released her and waved at one of the smaller tables.

'Sit down,' he said in a genial voice that she disliked at once. 'Let's get acquainted.'

Meenakshi sat, stacking her books on the table in front of her.

'My name is Varo, as I expect you have been informed.' He took the seat at the head of the table. 'What else do you know about me?'

Meenakshi hesitated. There was nothing to be gleaned from Varo's appearance. His clothes, although made of the fine, shimmering silk that everyone in Melucha seemed to wear, were simple. There was no signet ring, no insignia of a noble house embroidered on his cuffs, but she'd already known that.

'You're the Prince's First Minister,' she ventured at last.

Varo smiled. 'That's a good place to start, recognizing your own lack of knowledge. But you can't be content with that. Every time you see people—meet them at a formal dinner, see them in the street—is a chance to learn something.'

Meenakshi made a valiant attempt to look interested.

'I can tell you something I've learnt about you already. You didn't try to find out anything about me, or anybody in Melucha, other than what Kalban told you. Two mistakes. First, you should always know the people around you. Second, I know Kalban is your friend, but you cannot rely solely on his judgement. He is as prone as the rest of us to unconscious bias.'

'Er,' said Meenakshi.

'You're now wondering how much trouble you'll be in if you open an unauthorized portal back home to Madh and step through it. I expect you'll be in none at all for the portal, since you'll be in Madh, but your uncle will still insist on your learning Political Science. You won't escape that. We can make this easier. I'm the first to admit I'm not much of a teacher. What do you want to talk about?'

'Who killed Kras?' Meenakshi asked promptly.

She knew Kalban and Chitralekha would have come to the question more circumspectly. The direct approach had always worked for her.

Varo studied her for a long moment.

'All right,' he said at last. 'Sometimes it's best to go straight to the heart of a problem. The most important part of Political Science is knowing people. So it is while investigating a murder. Since you've asked, let's pursue this exercise. Who do *you* think killed Kras?'

'You were sitting next to him. But Kalban says that means you didn't kill him, because then you'd have made certain you were sitting far away, preferably in another country.'

'Maybe. Or maybe, knowing most people would take my proximity as a sign of my innocence, I placed myself beside him in as incriminating a position as possible. As it happens, I didn't kill him . . . You shouldn't believe me. If I *had* killed him, I wouldn't tell you. How would you go about investigating a murder?'

'It would have been easier to investigate if he'd been killed by magic. Everybody's magic is different. You can figure out who cast a spell. *Anyone* can put hemlock in a cup.'

'Whoever did this left no magical residue. That's true. There are other traces that can identify the perpetrator just as accurately. Take the circumstances of the murder. Find out about the people involved. You'll know who could have done it but didn't, and who couldn't have done it . . . and, in the end, who *did* it. What do you know about the people who were there? Start with the visitors. What do you know about Rati and Dev?'

'Rati is rich and powerful and she wants Abhinav to be the next ruler. And Dev paints elephants that look like bears and swans that look like a volcano.'

'You can't sum a human being up in a sentence,' said Varo. 'I'll give you a beginning. Melucha, as you might be aware, follows the principle of primogeniture. The firstborn inherits the estate in its entirety. Any other children receive an education and enough of a bequest to set them up in a respectable field. Rati was the youngest of five. When she was a child, her parents spoke to her about a profession. She told them she would have no need of one. It was laughable. A secondborn might arrange for a convenient accident . . . But Rati's oldest brother was twenty, fourteen years older than she was, and there were three others after him.'

'What did she do?'

'Nobody knows. Her oldest brother was killed in a freak accident a few days later. He was out in his boat and a giant wave washed him overboard. Rati was at home learning how to take two apples away from six apples. She couldn't have had anything to do with it. Her other siblings, for one reason and another, refused the inheritance. One much preferred the merchant navy, and another declared her lifelong ambition to retire to the country and grow wildflowers. In the end, Rati was the only one left.'

Meenakshi, despite herself, was interested.

'What about Dev?'

'Dev . . . Nobody understood why Rati chose *him*. I don't deny that he may have sterling qualities—he's loyal, for one thing, and he knows how to keep his mouth shut. But Rati is an ambitious woman, and Dev isn't the sort of man who could help her in that way. He was a commoner, and a middling artist. Maybe I'm doing her an injustice and she really fell in love.'

But I don't think so went unsaid.

'So Rati is ambitious and . . . killed her brother and got three other siblings out of the way so she could inherit the family estate.'

'You missed the point of the second part of the story. Rati was young, rich and powerful. There was no reason for her to marry a penniless artist when she could have had her choice of anyone in Melucha. But there was every reason for a penniless artist to marry a rich woman so he could spend his time on bad art instead of worrying about earning a living. So you see, Dev, if anything, was more ambitious . . . and just as successful.'

'What does this have to do with Kras?'

'Ambition drives human endeavour. We want to know more than we did yesterday, and be better, and so we learn and create. We never stop working towards something better than the present.' He paused. 'And sometimes, when the things we've worked so hard for are in danger, we do regrettable things to keep them safe.'

'Rati's estate?'

'Oh, no. But would someone like her—or Dev—be content with an estate, when the world is so wide and full of things to own? Kalban can tell you more details of this, but you are aware that Kras was his tutor, and Abhinav's?'

'Yes . . .'

'And was dishonourably discharged for accepting money from Rati to provide her with confidential information about his students?'

'Why would she care?'

'Did you learn nothing from what I just told you? Rati thinks ahead. One day either Kalban or Abhinav will be Prince of Melucha. Rati has a daughter a year younger than Abhinav. If, in the fullness of time, she should grow friendly with one of the sons of the present Prince Regnant, Rati wants to be certain that it's the *right* son.'

'Oh.' Meenakshi digested that silently. 'And she's decided Abhinav is the right one.'

'She's not the only one who thinks so. Abhinav reminds people of his father. The Prince has provided Melucha with several years of stable rule, and has done so without needing to resort to wholesale slaughter. Abhinav would have been the more popular choice in any case. To make matters worse, Kalban inherited his mother's magical abilities. There have been very few rulers in the history of Melucha who have had such . . . gifts. They all eventually had to be . . . put down . . . for the common good. Kalban might be different, but who knows?'

Chapter VI

'We have a problem,' Chitralekha announced. 'Nobody wants to talk to me.'

Meenakshi stared at her in mute astonishment. She had had a trying day. After telling her about Rati and Dev, Varo had changed the subject to the most effective way to get information from people one didn't know very well. He had taken on a variety of roles such as 'Maharaja's emissary', 'ambassador from Vraja' and 'person who has been chased by griffon and wants to file a complaint' and had forced Meenakshi to make small talk with him in each of those capacities.

'How is that a *problem*?' Meenakshi asked, finding her voice at last. 'How do you *do* it?'

'Ignore her,' Kalban said. 'She had a difficult time with Varo today.'

'What happened?' Chitralekha asked, perking up.

'He doesn't like *facts*,' said Meenakshi. 'You know the griffons, right? They're gentle. *And* they're in the vaults. If someone gets chased by them it can only be one of those idiots who sneaks down and pokes them with sticks to see if they'll react—or a thief, of course. Either way, someone who was asking for it.'

'Do people sneak into the vaults to see the griffons?'

'It's become quite a fad. Uncle Asamanjas is frustrated. He thought they'd keep thieves *away* from the vaults. He didn't anticipate that they'd encourage sightseers to break into them. There are plenty of warning signs and if people *will* ignore them . . .'

'Never mind,' Kalban said. 'Varo should have known better. As for you,' he added to Chitralekha, 'people in Melucha don't trust beings from the Inter-realm. I could have told you that. In fact, I *did* tell you that.'

'That's all very well, but someone needs to speak to Rati and Dev, and to Kras's wife—and no, it can't be you. You're a suspect. All right, maybe you didn't do it,' she went on hastily, forestalling Kalban's objection. 'That won't hold with Rambha. The whole point of going to this trouble is to *avoid* bringing her into the Mortal Realm.'

'All right,' Kalban said. 'What do you want to do?'

'I want to take Meenakshi to meet Rati.'

'No. She's not going into the city proper. We can invite Rati here.'

'That's not the same thing. We need to see Rati where *she* feels comfortable. She's likelier to talk.'

'Are you *insane*?'

'I'm sure Meenakshi won't turn anyone into a tortoise. Will you turn anyone into a tortoise?'

Meenakshi gave the matter her consideration. 'Not without provocation,' she said at last. 'If there *is* a reason . . . I've been discussing a new modification for size with Father so it would be interesting, and of academic importance–'

'You *see*?' Kalban said.

'Yes, I know Meenakshi's unpredictable. So do Rati and Dev, I expect. They'll know better than to offer provocation and I'll make it quick. There's no other way. They aren't practitioners of magic and therefore not covered under the Inter-Realm Accord. They don't *have* to cooperate with me. For the same reason, I can't enter their home uninvited or . . . any of *that* sort of thing. Rati *is* curious about Meenakshi. She wouldn't speak to me, but she hinted that if I brought Meenakshi, she'd let us in.'

'What happens when she's broken five different clauses of Section 39 and I have to sort out paperwork for days?'

'What happens if we can't solve this and Rambha decides to establish a Court of Inquiry in your library?'

Kalban paused, thought, and said, 'Fine.' Before Chitralekha could look too pleased, he added, 'I'm coming with you.'

'No, I thought I explained–look, I'll show you the Investigative Protocol Manual if you don't believe me.'

'No need, I've already read it. I won't say anything unless it looks like Meenakshi is going to cause us a lot of unnecessary trouble. I won't talk to your suspects at all. That satisfies the terms of the manual.'

'I suppose so,' said Chitralekha grudgingly. 'When can we do it?'

'Tomorrow afternoon, after Meenakshi's lessons.'

'All right. I want to search the palace this evening anyway. And yes,' she added, forestalling Kalban's question, 'that *is* covered under the Inter-Realm Accord. You and your mother live here.'

'None of us would be idiot enough to keep incriminating evidence here.'

'Good. You have nothing to worry about.'

Chitralekha looked around Kalban's well-appointed apartments with a fastidiously wrinkled nose. Meenakshi agreed with her: there *was* something odd about the room, though she couldn't put her finger on it.

She wasn't expecting Chitralekha's complaint.

'Marble sculptures in a bedroom! I've never heard of such a thing!'

Meenakshi laughed. 'And you with your palaces full of scandalous statuary! Kalban's only got a few nymphs, decorously robed and accompanied by suitable woodland creatures.'

'I've told you not to give too much credence to the geography books. The white marble in the Inter-Realm is for mortal consumption. They expect it, and we need them to keep believing in us, so . . .' She shuddered. 'Where are you going to start?'

'Where am *I* going to start? Aren't *you* searching?'

'Oh, no, this is you,' said Chitralekha. 'This, and Persis's room. I'll do the other two.'

'Why?'

'Because I don't want to get in the way of a magical booby-trap. You can sort those out.'

'Why do you care about booby-traps? You're invulnerable in the Mortal Realm.'

'A common belief, but not true. We're immune to mortal illnesses and poisons, but haven't you read the ballads about Alban knights who went around slaying unnatural creatures?'

'But the gods—'

'Yes, the gods *are* invulnerable. For the rest of us it's more of a guideline, and one that can be broken by someone with sufficient determination and the right sort of enchanted sword. We can't *die*, but we can be made too weak to maintain a corporeal form in the Mortal Realm.'

'This is *Kalban*. He doesn't booby-trap things.'

'You might find that Kalban does things in Melucha he wouldn't dream of doing in Madh.'

Meenakshi shook her head, but she went to the desk all the same. A quick spell revealed that it was indeed enchanted . . . to cover the fingers of any opener in a fine mist of red ink.

'How unoriginal,' Meenakshi muttered. She triggered the trap from a safe distance. The ink spattered onto the light blue velvet of Kalban's chair. 'I suppose that's what happens if the administration doesn't have an open mind about using magic to protect your privacy.'

'Will that come out?' Chitralekha asked. 'It looks permanent.'

'Kalban shouldn't have set such an obvious trap. Seeing it every day will be a lesson to him to use some finesse.'

Meenakshi went through the contents of the desk. There was nothing of note: her own last letter from Madh, complete with a diagram of her Alchemy experiment; her uncle's, considerably longer and with a page and a half of postscripts; and the minutes of the last Privy Council meeting, which had apparently been full of dull people making monotonous speeches about regulating scorpion breeding.

'No,' Chitralekha said, when Meenakshi reported her findings. 'We couldn't have expected to find anything here. Everyone would have been prepared for a search. They would have taken care to leave their rooms bare.'

And that was when Meenakshi realized what was odd.

'He *has* left it bare!' she exclaimed. 'Not just of evidence, of *everything*.'

'What are you talking about? The room's anything *but* bare. Did you not notice the stags on either side of the doorway? And the Maiden with Water Pot by the window?'

'And the row of laughing men on the mantelpiece,' Meenakshi said. 'Yes, but that's it. All very nice and artistic, no doubt–'

Chitralekha scoffed.

'All right, what *some* people might consider artistic,' Meenakshi amended. 'Did you see Kalban's study in Madh?'

'No,' said Chitralekha. 'Why?'

'It was full of *trappings*. A fire blazing on the hottest days so he could have a cauldron emitting noxious green fumes, jars of preserved Cryobotany specimens, stacks of joss sticks . . . That sort of thing. You could barely see through the fug of incense.'

'He *is* the type who likes to project an atmosphere,' agreed Chitralekha. 'And he's doing that here, too.'

'Stags and little laughing men?'

'It's not the *same* atmosphere. In Madh he was an apprentice sorcerer. Here he's Prince-heir, and he wants to retain his position.'

'He may be Prince-heir, but he's still a sorcerer. And Kalban isn't the sort of person who could be a sorcerer without the paraphernalia.' Meenakshi looked around. 'This is the sort of palace to have hidden rooms, isn't it?'

'The Maiden with the Water Pot,' Chitralekha said.

'That would be too obvious.'

'So?' Chitralekha crossed the room with quick strides. 'Weren't you complaining that he laid a trap a child could spot?'

'And weren't *you* afraid of triggering traps?' Meenakshi asked, as Chitralekha began running her hands over the statue.

'Oh. Yes. I'm not touching it.' Chitralekha stopped. 'What do you think?'

'You're right. Anyone who could come up with that red ink ridiculousness is bound to have put the hidden button in the Maiden with the Water Pot.'

'Really?'

'No, and in any case it would have been the architect who put in the hidden room, not Kalban. That's the only statue that's part of the original décor. It's carved from one of the pillars.'

It took some searching. No architect who earned his commission in Melucha would make secret rooms easy to find. At last, Chitralekha discovered that turning one of the rings on the Maiden's toes caused an infinitesimal jerk in a panel above the row of laughing men. When pressed, there was the customary grinding sound, and the wall beside the bed rolled down.

Meenakshi's eyes widened at the sight of what lay beyond. 'That is *not* real.'

'He does seem to have overdone it.'

'Over*done* it?' Meenakshi strode into the room. It was bathed in a weird green light. Something unpleasant was oozing down the inside walls. There was a strong smell of bitumen. 'This isn't *overdoing* it.'

'Look, I know this isn't what you're used to in Madh . . .'

'It's not what anyone should be used to anywhere!' Meenakshi waved a hand around. 'Just *look* at it. This isn't trinkets gathered to build up the atmosphere so people feel like they're getting real magic. This is . . . wrong. Unnatural.'

Chitralekha looked. The jars lining the walls were filled, not with plant specimens, but with *things* she didn't want to name. There were scorpions whose stings were so large they would never have been able to walk, snakes with huge staring eyes the size of her fist and fangs like daggers–

She shuddered.

'And *this*,' muttered Meenakshi, who had gone to the rickety bookshelf and was going over the titles. 'I've seen Kalban's bookshelf. He didn't own a single one of these books in Madh. I've never heard of some of them! *One Hundred Ways to Kill . . . Undetectable Magical Murder* . . . This is . . .'

'What?'

'This isn't Kalban's room,' Meenakshi said in sudden realization. 'There are no residues.'

'Are you sure?'

'Yes. There hasn't been magic in here for days, maybe for months. Maybe never.'

'Kalban might not have had time. There's been a lot happening.'

'That's impossible. Besides . . .' Meenakshi indicated the shelves. 'Look at the dust on everything. Oh, yes, I know he could conjure some for the look of the thing, but what's the point? He must have some other room for his magic.'

'We'll ask him when we're done,' said Chitralekha. 'Do you want to look around here?'

'*No.* Let's shut it and go, and if Kalban lets me I'll burn it all with magical fire tomorrow. Who's next?'

Abhinav's apartment was even more liberally supplied with robed nymphs carrying a variety of pots, ewers and baskets. One was making a garland of jasmine blossoms. Despite her evident distaste, Chitralekha took the search on herself, leaving Meenakshi free to leaf through a copy of *The Traveller's Guide to Gathering Poisonous Fungi* she found on the bookshelf.

'Do you suppose he really travels that much?' she asked Chitralekha. 'Most of this is about remembering to wear gloves when you pick purple mushrooms in the Eastern Isles. But it's a myth that their poison can penetrate the skin. Mother told me.'

'I imagine the book is for show,' Chitralekha did not look up from her examination of a dozen essays on the history of civil rights in Melucha. Meenakshi wondered if Abhinav had taken years of homework out of the schoolroom just to annoy them.

Then she wondered why they weren't searching the schoolroom.

'Don't be silly,' Chitralekha said when she asked. 'Nobody's going to leave anything incriminating in the schoolroom.'

'You said they wouldn't leave anything incriminating in their bedrooms, either.'

'If you're asking whether we're looking for a detailed plan of action and the bill of purchase for the hemlock, no, it's unlikely we'll find those. But we may understand the psychology of our suspects better. For instance, we know now that Kalban is either on the path to becoming a terrifying dark sorcerer or remarkably incurious about secret chambers opening from his bedroom.'

Shrugging, Meenakshi went back to her book.

An intake of breath from Chitralekha made her look up. 'What is it? A signed confession?'

'Not to murder. But this is *interesting*. Look.'

She pushed a sheaf of paper across the table. At first Meenakshi thought it was another essay, and wondered why Chitralekha felt the need to add to the reading list to which Varo had already condemned her.

Then she read the first paragraph.

'Melucha passed a law preventing a magician from taking the throne?'

'They've not passed it, but it's being discussed by the Privy Council. Even Kras weighed in. No wonder Kalban thinks people are plotting against him. It says the proposal came four months ago—very soon after Kalban came back.'

'Kalban didn't say anything about it.'

'He probably thinks if he pretends it isn't happening, it won't happen.' Chitralekha took the document back. 'Abhinav left this here for us to find. I wonder . . .' She hesitated. 'I suppose it's impossible that Kalban did it?'

'Kalban? *Murder* someone?'

'If he didn't use magic, it might not be a violation of the Inter-Realm Accord—and maybe he thought in Melucha it doesn't matter.'

'It's just a few steps from hemlock in the tea to a necromancer cackling in a tower. Kalban knows that. I think he liked Kras, but even if he didn't, he wouldn't have poisoned him.'

Chitralekha looked unconvinced, but she returned to her work. So, a moment later, did Meenakshi.

And then stopped.

'What?' asked Chitralekha.

'What would you say if I said I found a bill of purchase for hemlock?'

'I would say you must be seeing things. Knowing you, I'd be wrong.' Chitralekha held out a hand. 'Let me see.'

Meenakshi handed it over.

'It's two weeks old,' Chitralekha noted. 'Which makes it even more unlikely that Abhinav would leave it tucked into a book on poisons. Still, I suppose we have to look into it.' She gave it back to Meenakshi. 'Keep it safe. We'll go look at the Prince and Princess's apartments. I hope there are no surprises there.'

As Chitralekha prophecied correctly and there *were* no surprises in the Prince and Princess's chambers, they were finished well in time for Meenakshi to argue with Gopali about how formally she was required to dress for dinner.

Chapter VII

Meenakshi wasn't sure how she sat through dinner. Mada's habit of playing with his bracelets was maddening. He fiddled with them between courses. He fiddled with them during courses. Meenakshi was astonished the others could stand it. She would gladly have risked drinking soup laced with hemlock, strychnine and Datura to have been spared the endless jingling.

Conversation was slow. It was possible that that was in deference to her, but from what Kalban had told her, she doubted it.

Perhaps, she thought with a sudden flash of insight, the interminable debate on the new tariffs on magical imports was because they didn't want to be overheard by Mada, Amar and Varo, all of whom were also at dinner.

Meenakshi turned her gaze to the court bard, who returned it with equal, if better concealed, curiosity.

There were no court bards in Madh. As far as she knew, there never had been. Poets and musicians were sometimes invited to perform at state dinners. A distraction might be required to fill awkward gaps in conversation, particularly if her father and the High Priest of the Sun God were both going to be present. Meenakshi couldn't imagine going through life being followed by someone whose sole job was to put everything she did into bland verse.

Persis caught her eye with a conspiratorial smile that determined Meenakshi to ask her, later, what the purpose of the court bard was.

There was a palpable sense of relief when the last course was cleared away. Since there were no guests, the family dispersed, and Meenakshi was free to take Kalban aside and demand an explanation of the hidden room.

'There's a hidden room?' he said. Then, with a hint of irritation, 'There's a hidden *room* in my room, and I've been going to the trouble of sneaking to the cellar when I needed to practice magic?'

'The *cellar*. I should have guessed.'

'Where's the secret room?'

'Chitralekha said she'd be waiting. We can show you.'

Kalban's reaction to the room was enough to convince Meenakshi that he truly hadn't known of its existence before. She would have expected him to have found it as a child. He'd gone around tapping every wall and door panel in Madh for weeks before he'd accepted that there were no hidden passages.

'I don't understand,' he muttered, staring at the horrifying specimens in the jars. 'It's like someone's been experimenting, but I don't see *why*.'

'How else would one get in here, if not through your room?' Chitralekha asked.

'I don't see how there can be another entrance. Every other wall has shelves. I need to see what's in *that* book. I don't think there's a copy in Madh.'

Meenakshi gestured at the shelf. *Undetectable Magical Murder* floated towards her. She borrowed Kalban's handkerchief to dust it thoroughly before she opened it.

Kalban peered over her shoulder. Chitralekha edged closer to have a look.

'I'll have to write to Father to be sure,' Meenakshi said, flicking through the pages of hideous diagrams as quickly as she could. 'Most of these spells have been discredited.'

'They're not real?' Chitralekha asked.

'Proved to be unqualified quackery years ago. Oh.' Meenakshi went back to the first page to look for the printer's mark. 'This book is twenty years old. Do you think it might be your mother's, from before she married your father?'

Kalban groaned. 'That wouldn't surprise me.'

'It doesn't matter. None of these spells does anything. It can't have anything to do with Kras's death.' She put the book back. 'I suppose . . .' She looked a little regretful. 'There wouldn't be much point looking at the rest, I'm sure. Unless . . .'

She hesitated and glanced at Chitralekha, who shrugged. 'Tell him, it doesn't matter. We need to go look in the kitchens anyway.'

'Tell me what?'

'We found a bill of purchase for hemlock in one of Abhinav's books.'

'The regulations have tightened,' Kalban said. 'And the black market in poisons has almost entirely dried up in the last few years. You can't get a bunch of hemlock from a pushcart at the street corner anymore. The Privy Council thinks it's better if they know what's happening. You can't buy a Class I poison without a record on both sides.'

'Why would Abhinav need a record of the seller?'

'He needs evidence of where he got it. How else can he file a complaint if it doesn't work as expected? But,' Kalban went on, 'as much as he infuriates me, and as likely as it is that he killed Kras, a bill of purchase isn't proof of that. Everyone has stores of hemlock.'

'Then the hemlock isn't important.'

'It isn't *conclusive*. What's alarming is *these* things.' Meenakshi shuddered again as she followed the direction of Kalban's gesture to the shelves of specimens. 'There's only a limited number of people in Melucha capable of Alchemy on this scale–'

'*No*,' Meenakshi said, realizing something.

'I'm telling you, there are very few people who could have done it.'

'No, no, not that. It's not Alchemy.' Meenakshi picked up one of the jars and examined its contents, making Kalban look at her with a mixture of alarm and disapproval.

'You're not going to try–'

'Don't be ridiculous, of course I'm not. It isn't Alchemy. There are no residues of magic in this room. It must be selective breeding . . .' Her fingers trailed along the row of scorpions. 'Starting at what must have been natural, if unusual, and increasing in size.'

Kalban looked relieved. 'You're right. It's nothing to worry about. There'll be new scorpion breeding regulations in force soon. Whoever did this will have to stop.'

'Maybe that's why they did stop . . . No, that doesn't make sense. They must have stopped some time ago. This room looks like nobody's set foot in it for years.'

Chitralekha said, 'I know you're all murderous psychopaths in Melucha, but why would anyone want to breed larger stings in scorpions?'

'More poison, I should think. Very few scorpions are capable of killing a healthy adult, and it's very difficult to get them. There are some physicians who believe scorpion venom in small doses might have medicinal benefits.'

'Someone thought scorpions weren't a sufficiently reliable murder weapon, and wanted to *remedy* the situation?'

'I don't know. It isn't important. Someone knew about this secret room, used it for his or her experiments, and had to stop . . . when I came back at the latest, but, as Meenakshi says, probably earlier. Maybe it was Abhinav. But the scorpion breeding laws haven't yet gone into force, so, however distasteful, it wasn't illegal.'

'Do you think Kras found out and Abhinav killed him so he wouldn't tell anyone?' Meenakshi asked.

'You're not hearing me. Even if Abhinav was using this room to breed scorpions, it wouldn't have mattered. It's not yet illegal. Do you suppose anyone in Melucha cares if people are experimenting with new ways to murder? Do *you* even read the Arcane Zoology Authorization Desk pamphlets anymore?'

'All right,' Chitralekha said. 'Don't argue. I want to go look at the kitchen and find out how it works. I want to know how easy it would have been for someone to poison Kras's tea before it went to the library.'

'But the head of the kitchen–'

'Drank it and suffered no ill effects. I know. Humour me.'

Mada the head of the kitchen staff, ruling his domain at the back of the palace, was a very different person from Mada the official food taster, who sat at the dining table, fiddled with his bracelets, and picked at his own fine meals as though they were a heel of four-day-old bread.

By the time they arrived, the palace staff had finished their dinner and were bustling about, some clearing the large table where they ate, others hurrying back to their duties. Mada was supervising the flurry of activity with a scowl fierce enough to belong to a carven warlord. His manner didn't change when he saw his visitors.

'You're here about the tea.' His manner couldn't have been less gracious if they'd been weevils he found in the wheat. 'Come. Let's get it over with.'

He favoured Chitralekha with a baleful glare, which surprised Meenakshi: most people in Melucha so far had treated the Dancer with civility, even if it was tempered by wariness.

He stalked ahead of them down the corridor. The air grew cool. 'It's no magic,' he said over his shoulder. 'Just excellent architecture. We channel in the breezes. They do wonders for temperature maintenance, particularly at night. The rooms are as far from sunlight as possible.'

‘Why is magic so highly regulated in Melucha?’ Meenakshi muttered.

‘It’s not just Melucha,’ Kalban told her. ‘There’s no other city in the Free Lands where magic is permitted on the streets. All practitioners have to be licensed and public spellcasting is banned—barring emergencies, of course.’

‘Isn’t it difficult to enforce?’

‘It used to be. But practitioners of magic are a very small percentage of the population everywhere but in Madh, and . . .’

‘I’ll explain,’ Chitralekha said. ‘Many, many years ago, before the Inter-Realm Accords, before a lot of things, there were some sorcerers and sorceresses who tried to make themselves dictators. The evil kind. Naturally, the damage of which they were capable was . . . extreme . . . even by the standards of evil dictators. Fewer dungeons and more hailstorms destroying the mango crop. We intervened as much as we could, but we’re not perfect, and there were enough incidents that people decided they’d had enough.’

‘There were armed protests,’ Kalban added. ‘People revolted. Magic can’t save you if hundreds of thousands of people are determined to put your head on a pike. When that happened enough times . . . The regulations are a way of making sure it doesn’t happen again.’

‘Except in Madh?’

‘There was the Academy. And the position of Master Sorcerer has historically been held in Madh as well, since it’s the hub of Inter-Realm traffic. That helped, because it meant there was some regulation, and enough practitioners of magic congregated there that they could keep a check on each other. That isn’t a perfect solution, but it’s held, by and large.’

'I would hate to interrupt the history lesson,' Mada said. 'Please don't hurry on *my* account. It isn't like I have dinner to plan.'

They had entered a large, dark room. It had no windows, but it somehow contrived to be airy. Large boxes lined the walls and were arranged in islands, with corridors allowing the passage of a single person at a time.

Mada manoeuvred through the rows and opened a box. There was an immediate strong, not entirely pleasant, smell of herbs. It didn't bother Meenakshi—it was no worse than an Alchemy lab—and she didn't suppose it bothered the kitchen staff, who must be used to strong smells.

Kalban peered into the box. 'There's just a little in the bottom.'

'It's what was left after Kras was dismissed. I ordered more when I heard he'd be coming back as tutor . . .' He cast a sidelong glance at Meenakshi. 'Maybe we should throw it away now. Or we could keep it for the court bard. I'm told he's been advised to take it for his throat, though he's never had it to my knowledge.'

'Wait, this is the *old* supply of tea? From before Kras was dismissed?'

'Don't ask me why it was kept. It's stale, which is generally undesirable. But if you were drinking *this* I don't suppose you'd notice.'

'It might be best to throw it away now,' Chitralekha said, peering in. 'If you've ordered more anyway . . .'

Meenakshi had never, in their admittedly short acquaintance, known Chitralekha to take an interest in the running of a mortal household. Celestial Dancers couldn't stomach mortal foods. She had heard more than one Sprite gloating over that; Sprites could not only consume mortal food, they had a particular gift for conjuring lavish feasts.

There had been one her father had Summoned—

Kalban nudged her. 'The head of the kitchen,' he said, 'was explaining what happened on the night Kras died.'

'Perhaps it's not very interesting to a young girl,' said Mada coldly.

'I want some of the tea to test,' Meenakshi said.

'That's already been done.'

'Not by me.'

'Of course. We've all heard of the . . . gifts . . . of the Master Sorcerer's daughter. I'm sure you'll solve the mystery before tomorrow's dawn.'

Apparently, Chitralekha wasn't the only one to whom Mada had an aversion.

Opening a small jar she had brought, Meenakshi bent to scoop up some of the tea. She was leaning halfway into the bin to do it, when Kalban seized her by the shoulders and pulled her back, upsetting the bin in the process.

'What are you *doing*?' she demanded furiously. 'I'm trying to get a clean sample!'

'No hope of that,' Kalban said, pulling her further away from the bin. 'See for yourself.'

There was a soft hiss, and a long dark shape slithered out of the bin. Meenakshi had a glimpse of eyes glittering like onyxes. Then it shot away to disappear into the shadows.

'Oh,' said Meenakshi. 'That's annoying.'

'You mean you didn't sense the snake?' Even in the shadowy lamplight, Meenakshi could see Mada's malicious smile. 'Apparently magic can't do everything, can it?'

'How long has it been in the bin?'

'I have no idea. That bin hadn't been opened for years.'

'It couldn't have lasted years without food,' said Kalban. 'It must have slipped in when they opened it to take Kras's tea. What happened that night?'

'I wish I could be helpful,' said Mada, who had evidently not been brought up to believe that the Goddess of Truth had thunderbolts in store for barefaced liars. 'I can't remember. One night is so much like another. I left the teapot, with a double scoop of this, on the tray with the wine carafe. That's all I know.'

'Could anyone have tampered with it while you were upstairs?' Meenakshi asked.

'My kitchen is not known for anarchy. The staff work in groups of three—groups whose composition changes every day—to prevent conspiracies of the very sort you must be imagining now. When the attendant on duty goes to collect the wine, at least two others accompany him.'

'Where was it kept?' asked Chitralekha.

Mada's glare would have reduced one of his under-cooks to helpless blubbering. Chitralekha smiled.

He led them out of the room, down a flight of stairs to another. This one was full of barrels and a musty grape smell.

'This is where we keep the wine that's ready for consumption.' He indicated a table in the middle of the room. 'The tray with the carafe is placed there before dinner. The attendant would have filled the carafe from one of the barrels. But the wine itself was untouched, so this hardly matters.'

'If the accompanying cooks were both peering into that corner trying to see if the attendant was poisoning the wine,' Meenakshi said, 'they might not have noticed if one of them slipped something into the tea.'

Mada's unblinking eyes were eerily bright. 'Quite right. But I drank the tea as well as the tutor, and, as you see, here I am. Now, I hate to seem inhospitable, but I have to earn my keep. If you have no further questions . . .' There was an infinitesimal pause, a warning that everything they ate was in Mada's purview, and one person had already died by poison. 'Shall we go up?'

Meenakshi found one final surprise waiting in her room. A letter had been pushed under the door. It bore her name but no indication of its source.

'Who delivered this?' she asked Gopali. 'Do you know?'

'No idea. Is it poisoned? Let me check.' She took it and examined the envelope. 'It seems all right.' She slit the envelope, shook out the letter, crumpled it without unfolding it, and then handed it to Meenakshi.

Meenakshi smoothed it out.

It had one line, in printed capitals.

WHO ASKED KRAS TO COME TO DINNER?

Meenakshi stared at it for a moment, and then passed it to Gopali.

'What do you think that's about?'

'Who *did* ask Kras to come to dinner?' Gopali said.

'Kalban did. Why?' Gopali looked at her. 'Oh no, you're not suggesting that *Kalban* murdered Kras? It's bad enough that Chitralekha is starting to suspect that he did.'

'If it weren't a possibility, Chitralekha wouldn't be here. But that's not the point. We'll know soon enough if he did. It's clear that someone *wants* you to think Kalban murdered Kras.'

'Should I tell Kalban? Warn him that someone's working against him?'

'There's no need. He's already adding more than his fair share of gloom to the atmosphere. Don't give him another reason to look like a tragic actor.'

CHAPTER VIII

Despite Gopali's advice, Meenakshi decided to tell Kalban about the letter when he came to her room after breakfast. As soon as she'd done it, she wished she'd listened to Gopali. Kalban responded with an intensity of expression that was almost more alarming than the hollow groan and forehead-clutching she'd expected.

'Do you have the letter?'

Meenakshi handed it over. Kalban barely glanced at it before he said, 'It's the same handwriting as one I got—I wrote to you about it, remember? Saying I should go back to Madh?'

'When you found a snake in your room? That was before Kras was killed.'

'Yes. If it's the same person . . .'

'Someone killed Kras just so they could frame you for the murder?' Meenakshi couldn't keep the scepticism out of her voice. 'Aren't there easier ways to get rid of people?'

'This would discredit me—make it nearly impossible for me to get support for the throne. If it weren't for the . . . *magic* . . . problem, the Privy Council would support me.' His voice was far less certain than the words. 'They're wavering already. This would settle it. This is why I didn't want to come back. Everyone's waiting for me to turn into a dark sorcerer.'

Meenakshi was fascinated by what she saw of the city on the carriage ride. Unlike Madh, the topography of which had the haphazardness of a city where a combination of engineering and magic had been used to put up buildings wherever there was a bit of space and the Urban Development Authority wouldn't nag you about blocking somebody's right of way, Melucha was laid out with geometrical precision. The spirals of cobblestone roads wrapping themselves around the hills seemed like a different, hypnotic magic.

'This is where the aristocrats live,' Chitralekha offered, as they rolled past ornate gates set in high walls. 'They don't want poor people looking into their gardens and becoming discontented by the lack of Maidens with Water Pots in their lives.'

'I still think this is a bad idea,' Kalban muttered. He was slouched in his seat, the curtain drawn across his window. 'Anything might happen.'

'You're here to see that it doesn't.'

'All we need is to meet one more practitioner of magic by the roadside and we'll be in violation of Section 39—'

'Here we are!' Chitralekha said.

The carriage had stopped before a set of gates decorated with whimsical patterns of vines and fruit. When they slid open, Meenakshi saw lush lawns bordered by rows of flowers. The grass was so even it looked like someone must have cut it with a ruler.

People in Melucha might dislike magic, but it was evident they didn't like things done the natural way, either.

The carriage drew up to a flight of marble steps where a white-haired man was waiting, watching with disapproval. It was hard to judge whether Kalban or Meenakshi came in for the greater share of his hostile glare.

He ushered them in with a gesture, hustling them through an entrance hall lined with Cavorting Woodland Maidens in several different hues of marble, into a sitting room. Meenakshi wouldn't have been surprised to learn the room was meant for the befuddlement of visitors: the air was hazy with incense and the upholstery and curtains were made of a deep red material that seemed to fill the room with a faint rosy glow. There was the same superfluity of carved nymphs that characterized the palace.

Meenakshi was tempted to turn the rosy glow into something eerie and green, but one look at Kalban's face decided her against it. There was nothing to do after that but sit and wish for a book.

The mistress of the house didn't keep them waiting long. They had barely been enough time for the disapproving gentleman to offer them wine, and for Kalban to refuse on everyone's behalf, when there were footsteps outside. A moment later, the doors were flung open, and Rati entered.

Meenakshi had seen women like her in Madh, usually coming and going from the spymaster's office. Although they claimed their primary aim was diplomacy, they tended to have four or five daggers hidden in various folds of their garments. Rati looked like she might disregard weapons and hit you over the head with one of the smaller nymphs.

She ignored both Kalban and Chitralekha, addressing herself directly to Meenakshi.

'I'm so glad to meet you at last. I've heard a great deal about you. There has been speculation about the real reason for your visit. Does this herald a new era of friendship in our relations with Madh?'

'Um,' said Meenakshi, since Kalban hadn't given her any prior coaching on answering questions about international relations.

'It is unfortunate that your visit to Melucha has been disrupted by this investigation.' Rati sounded like she had seen a large discoloured stain on one of the red curtains. 'It's a minor matter, but I understand that Madh takes a more conservative view of these little inconveniences. And yet it has a far more licentious attitude with regard to magic. I've always thought that revealing.'

'A man was murdered,' Meenakshi said, finding her voice at last. 'Isn't that more than an inconvenience?'

'To Kras, perhaps. I see no reason for an Inter-Realm investigation. Kras had a lifelong habit of meddling in matters that didn't concern him. This was the inevitable and long-delayed consequence. If it hadn't involved Kalban and Persis, it would have been investigated, *quietly*, by the Palace Guard. The Prince would have exiled the perpetrator, arranged a generous settlement for the widow, and we wouldn't be talking about it days later.'

'The Palace Guard doesn't know who did it.'

'Who told you that? There's no proof, but it's clear who did it. And I sympathize. Kras . . . it's only surprising that this didn't happen sooner.'

'Because he meddled in matters that didn't concern him.'

'You're a quick learner.'

'How did he meddle in matters that didn't concern him?'

'*And* you're direct. How . . . refreshing.'

'I did warn you,' Chitralekha piped up. 'She doesn't do small talk.'

'So you did,' said Rati. 'Very well. I can adjust. I'll answer your question, if you answer mine. Kalban, do you want to leave the room? This might be awkward.'

'If you're going to ask her about me, go ahead. She's not going to hold back to spare my feelings.'

'We heard alarming rumours, even here in Melucha, of events in Madh a few months ago. Kalban's friend Avi has been talkative.'

'If you mean the Thoughtform,' said Meenakshi, 'there was no need for alarm. There were some people who thought they could play with things they didn't understand.'

'Avi was expelled from the Academy. I thought that was a sign that his actions were regarded as a serious violation of the Code of Sorcery . . . or perhaps that playing with things you don't understand is the first step on a dangerous path. He wasn't allowed to stay in the city proper.'

'The Master of the Academy didn't ask for *that*.'

'The Privy Council did. I wasn't on it at the time, but I would have agreed. He was too great a risk. That brings me to my question. We were *assured* that Kalban had nothing to do with it.'

Meenakshi glanced at Kalban. 'We eliminated it.'

'You and Kalban?'

'Not *alone*. We had help.'

'The Master Sorcerer didn't have to get involved,' Chitralekha volunteered.

'Avi is his friend. How certain were you that Kalban hadn't been involved in making the . . . creature?'

'*Kalban*?' Meenakshi shook her head. 'Kalban doesn't like to experiment with Alchemy. Kalban never even Summoned a *yaksha* without a reason.' With a sharp glance at Rati, she added, 'I'm beginning to see why.'

'We'll talk more on that subject later. Now, about Kras . . . I was going to say Kalban could have told you, but most of it happened before he was born and of course he spent so many years in Madh. I don't suppose he knows the details. Have you met his wife yet?'

'Kras's wife? No.'

'Angana has fallen on difficult times since her youth.' She waved her hands at the opulence around them, which Meenakshi took to mean that Angana's family had once inhabited a similar marble-infested mansion. 'She'll have a pension as the widow of a former Royal Tutor. And I believe she has an income of her own. She won't *starve*. But her parents were among the most influential people in Melucha. They intended that she should marry the Prince.'

'Kalban told me *you* wanted to marry the Prince.'

Kalban opened his mouth, shut it at a look from Chitralekha, and buried his head in his hands.

'Don't worry,' Rati said in his direction. 'I'm enjoying this conversation. It was years ago. Yes, I did want to marry the Prince. Everyone did. You must realize that when there's a young Prince or Princess—or heir, of course—not yet spoken for, everyone of a suitable age wants to be in the running. I'm not bitter. It worked out for the best. Better Persis in the palace than Persis making navigation difficult for the ships at the mouth of the Nati. Besides, in some ways her presence has been invaluable.'

'Go on with the story,' Chitralekha said.

'I thought the point of Meenakshi's being in Melucha was to learn how statecraft works when you can't terrorize people with magic fire.'

Meenakshi drew a breath to describe the total lack of magic fire in Madh, as an instrument of persuasion or otherwise, but Chitralekha nudged her.

'At the time, the Prince was the Prince-heir,' Rati went on. 'It was his mother's reign. I mean no offence,' she added to Kalban, 'when I say she wasn't a strong ruler. She had always been frail and had suffered through a severe illness. It was a matter of time. Although the Privy Council was in Shel's favour, there was a minority supporting the claims of a distant cousin. When it became clear that the Prince wouldn't marry Angana, her parents put their support behind the cousin.'

'Where does Kras come into this?'

'Kras was the Royal Tutor. Shel's tutor. Angana's parents enlisted him in their cause. His position gave him some unique advantages, as I'm sure you can imagine.'

'She means he was close to the Prince and could have put hemlock in *his* tea if necessary,' Chitralekha supplied.

'Quite. The details aren't important. When the dust had settled, the Prince was on the throne, Angana's parents and brother were exiled, and the family estates were forfeit. Angana was regarded as having had nothing to do with it, so she was allowed to remain. She found some quiet work that would keep her busy—or so we were all told. At any rate she stayed out of politics. She married Kras, whose involvement went undetected—although there were rumours—and who therefore continued in his sinecure as Royal Tutor.'

'If his involvement went undetected, how do *you* know?'

Rati smiled. 'I make it my business to know things. Kras had a history of meddling in affairs that were none of his business. He didn't suffer any consequences *then*. Is it any surprise that he did now?'

'Who do you think did it?'

'Does it matter? Anyone might have done it. My point is that it's not . . .' Rati waved a hand again. 'It's not an *important* murder. Kras was a forgotten relic of a bygone dispute. Nobody's likely to have trusted him enough to give him sensitive information *now*. It doesn't change the future.'

'It changes Kras's future,' Meenakshi pointed out. 'He doesn't have one anymore.'

'Do you remember what happened that night?' Chitralekha said, when it looked like Rati intended to elaborate on the subject of the insignificance of Kras's future.

'The night of the murder? At dinner, you mean? We sat around the table. Nobody could have poisoned anything, nobody got up.'

'And afterwards?'

'In the library? Everyone was walking around. I don't remember the details.'

Meenakshi knew that was a lie. Rati struck her as the sort of woman who would pay attention to everyone's activities, and mention them at inconvenient times, such as when one was trying *not* to draw attention to the fact that one had been reading a book on Experimental Summoning the week before the mysterious appearance of a pair of djinn in one's uncle's study.

She tried not to feel too pleased with herself over the realization.

Rati was still talking.

'. . . and I don't know why Dev wastes his time. It's art; you can't *force* people to like it. But there it is. He insists on trying to persuade Persis to sit for a portrait. If you don't have any other questions, I have a busy day.'

The dismissal was clear.

'We're not finished,' said Chitralekha. 'As much as I sympathize with your eagerness to get rid of us, we still need to speak to your husband.'

'Dev? I assure you Dev can't help you.'

'Meenakshi can answer another question for you.'

Meenakshi opened her mouth to say that she hadn't signed up for unnecessary interrogation about magical incidents in Madh, but Rati forestalled her with, 'Fine. Alone.'

This time it was Kalban who objected. 'No. No, no, we've discussed this. I'm not risking a diplomatic incident, Asamanjas will never let me forget it—'

'Don't be absurd,' said Rati. 'I'm not such an idiot as you make me sound. Nor, I'm sure, is Meenakshi. We can conduct a civil conversation for a few minutes without anything unpleasant happening.'

'But—'

'Leave it,' Chitralekha advised, getting to her feet and tugging Kalban up with her. 'Let's wait in the hall. I saw a delightful but highly inaccurate depiction of the Goddess of Truth that I want to examine in detail. Perhaps we could leave Dev some notes to help with his next attempt.' Kalban, still protesting, was hauled out after her.

'Look,' Meenakshi heard her saying as they left the room, 'she's *here* to learn how to deal with people, isn't she? Right, let her learn. We've warned Rati. She can't complain if she gets turned into a frog.'

Rati laughed, seeming less guarded and more affable. Meenakshi knew, from Kalban's lectures, that it was time to be alarmed.

She wasn't.

Rati made no move to offer Meenakshi wine, tea, water or any other beverage that would give her the opportunity of heeding Kalban's strenuous advice to refuse all refreshment.

'I should tell you something about how Melucha works,' she said. 'I can see how shocked you are by my practical approach to Kras's murder. If your knowledge of our city is from Kalban's stories, you must think it's a minor miracle that the Prince has ruled for twenty years and accumulated a total of zero knives in the back.'

'Hasn't one in three rulers of Melucha died of unnatural causes?'

'That's a very convenient statistic. It keeps changing to suit the occasion . . . Do you know what people in Melucha say about Madh? That it's full of *unnatural* creatures from the Inter-Realm, that magic runs wild and uncontrolled.'

'The Magical Activities Legislative Board keeps making new laws to keep it in check.'

'All I conclude from that information is that it needs to be kept in check. Let me put it another way. In Melucha, power—political power—is ephemeral. You might lose everything in an instant. That's a fact of life. If you want power, you must *fight* for it.'

'Why would you want it?'

'*I* don't want the throne, which, I think, is what you mean. But I *do* want to know that I can trust the person *on* the throne to make sensible decisions.'

'Decisions *you* like, you mean.'

'I try to be objective. Kalban's father is an excellent administrator. That's why he's been allowed to rule for so long. But you have to expect the occasional cup of poisoned tea in Melucha, like you have to expect the occasional horde of djinn in Madh. Those who don't want to participate in machinations and intrigues are left alone. Royal Tutors are meant to educate their charges, whoever they may be, with impartiality. Kras chose to get involved. He knew the risks.'

'Why does that matter? Chitralekha still needs to know who did it.'

'Kalban has been away from home for a very long time. He's been away long enough to treat venomous beasts with far more alarm than they deserve. You might want to keep that in mind. This brings me to my question.'

'Yes?' Meenakshi said warily.

'Some magicians are evil. I don't mean simply that they're charlatans peddling fake cures for the plague. They lose themselves in their magic and do terrible things.'

Meenakshi nodded. She knew that danger. Everyone who learnt magic knew it. No matter how careful you were, no matter how closely the Dancers monitored you or you watched yourself—and magicians who didn't want to be evil watched themselves every single day—you might fail.

'Is it likely to happen to Kalban?' Rati asked.

Meenakshi considered the question. It wasn't one to be answered lightly. 'It's not impossible,' she said at last. 'It never is—not for anyone. But Kalban is . . . he's the last person I would think might . . . stray.'

'What happens to people who *stray*?'

'The Magical Activities Legislative Board. If it gets *too* bad, the Dancers.'

'Would *you*?'

'Would I what?'

'If Kalban became evil, here in Melucha, more than the Dancers could handle, and somebody told you, would you be willing to do something about it?'

'It doesn't happen often,' Meenakshi said slowly. 'If it did—to anyone—yes. There wouldn't be much choice in the matter.'

'Good. I needed to know. Now let's call your friends back in. I'll have someone fetch Dev.'

Meenakshi took an immediate dislike to the man who entered the room after Rati left. Kalban had said Dev was an artist, so she supposed he couldn't be entirely without a soul, but there was no sign of it in his eyes. They glittered like a reptile's—though Meenakshi didn't know why people who were inhuman were accused of being reptilian. Reptiles minded their own business and didn't attack other reptiles for no reason.

'Rati says I have to talk to you.' Dev's manner was unpleasant. 'Get on with it.'

Chitralekha didn't try to charm him. It would probably be a violation of some subclause of the Inter-Realm Accord. Instead she said, as briskly as Meenakshi herself might have done, 'We won't take much of your time. Tell us what happened on the night of Kras's murder.'

Dev leaned back in his chair. 'I didn't want to go. I wish now I hadn't. Formal dinners are a frightful bore. I wanted to work on my new piece. It's called *Anonymity*, one of a pair. The other one is *Transience*. Rati insisted I had to go.' He smiled.

Meenakshi thought, all things considered, that a crocodile's grin might be more unnerving, but it would be a close contest.

'Melucha is an artist's paradise if your work is appreciated by the right people. If you get the approval of the Council of Art, people give you commissions and exhibit your work in the Grand Gallery. Otherwise you might languish in obscurity for years.'

'The Council of Art doesn't approve of you?' asked Meenakshi.

'They don't understand my work. They *do* understand that my wife is a major patron of the Gallery. As a consequence, my life revolves around doing the things Rati insists on.'

'Like formal dinners.'

'I don't like to involve myself in the . . . unpleasantness. Negative energy is bad for the creative spirit. But she was very firm about this one. I thought I might at least see the new mural in the dancing hall. That would have made it worthwhile. But we never went there.'

He looked accusingly at Kalban.

'Go on,' said Chitralekha, who had appointed herself official reiner-in of tangents. 'You went to the palace . . . and then . . . ?'

'We met that silly poet first. That should have told me the evening would be a disaster. The old idiots Kras and Varo were there. We had dinner. What more do you want? I was bored out of my mind. After dinner we went to the library, where there are a few passable paintings. We had some wine and looked at them. Kras went to bed early. Then we could leave.'

'Were you surprised to hear he'd been killed?'

Dev barked out another mirthless laugh. 'Surprised to hear there'd been a murder? In *Melucha*? All the same . . .' he went on, 'I wasn't particularly *expecting* anything to happen to Kras.'

'No?'

'It's such a waste of time. Who could feel sufficiently threatened by that senile has-been? He was a dried-out remnant of an ancient plot who had nothing to do but preach cautionary tales of the ways he had failed.'

'Somebody *did* feel threatened enough to poison him.'

'And you're wasting your time worrying about it because you think he was *important*? It was probably his wife. Anyone who had to put up with Kras droning on about the theory of government day after day and didn't feel a little murderous would have to be . . .' He glanced at Chitralekha. 'Forgive me, I was going to say inhuman, but *you'd* have wanted to kill him too. Angana is harmless, though. Her parents and brother plotted a coup right under her nose and she had no idea. I think Kras killed himself.'

'Why would he do that?'

'Maybe the truth about him was going to come out and he couldn't stand the shame.'

'That sounds very unlikely,' Chitralekha said. 'Do people in Melucha prefer death to dishonour?'

'They tend to get murdered before they have the chance to make a choice. People are people. What did Kras have left to live for?'

CHAPTER IX

Gopali was waiting when Meenakshi got back to her bedroom. She was pale and breathing quickly. Having worked with Meenakshi for years, Gopali was immune to what most people would have considered serious shocks. Had she found that a bored yaksha had disarranged the papers on the desk and was standing in the corner of the room waiting for instructions, she would have shrugged and gone about her business.

'What is it this time?' Meenakshi asked. 'Venomous toads?'

'No such luck,' Gopali said. 'That odious man has been here asking after your whereabouts.'

'Which odious man?'

'Varo. The tutor.'

'Is he odious? Kalban seems to think he's all right, other than passing information to the Privy Council.'

'Since when do *we* think people are *all right* simply because Kalban does? There's something wrong with Varo. I can feel it. If you ask me, *he's* the one Chitralekha is after.'

'Why would he want to kill Kras?' Meenakshi was unaccustomed to being the voice of reason, especially with Gopali, who was normally the one insisting that she had to go to the Inter-Realm Liaison Bureau's annual dinner; yes, she had to, even if she couldn't stand Nalini, and furthermore she couldn't take a book to read under the table.

'From what I've heard, he was Varo's major political rival.'

'Dev said Kras was a has-been with no influence–'

'Who's Dev? Never mind, I'm sure he's a liar like everyone else here.' Gopali looked gloomy. 'I do *not* like this place, and I promise you I'll be telling your uncle so when I go back. I agree it was unfortunate that you were failing Political Science and Negotiation, but your father was the first person in history to get negative marks on the Negotiation course and we're getting on fine in Madh, aren't we?'

'I tried to tell Uncle Asamanjas. He wouldn't listen.'

'It can't be helped. We're here now. I suppose the only thing to do is to endure it until we can leave. Can't you just *apply* yourself to statecraft for once so we can get out of here sooner? You're capable of learning every other subject; I refuse to believe you're incurably dim at this one.'

'What did he want?'

'Who? Asamanjas?'

'*Varo*. You said he was here.'

'Oh. Yes. He left some books for you. He wants you to read the first two chapters of each before your next lesson.' Gopali waved at a stack of books on the desk. They looked like the sort of books that would be filled with boring descriptions of the nature of human needs, accompanied by diagrams like spiderwebs. That was what had put Meenakshi off Political Science in the first place.

'My next lesson is tomorrow.'

'Lesson after that. Does it matter?'

'Will he notice if I just read the first sentence of each page?'

'Don't try it. If he fails you and makes you start again we'll be stuck here longer.'

'You don't like Melucha, do you?'

'I'm used to Madh. If someone does set a nightmare monster on you, it's an accident—or a prank, if you're a student at the Academy. Here when they put a scorpion in your bed they intend for you to die.'

'What happened?'

'Why should anything have happened?'

'In all the time I've known you, you've never been this bothered about anything. What aren't you telling me?'

Gopali scowled. 'I reserve the right to ban you from going.' She held out a fist that was clenched around a sheet of paper that looked as though she had, at some point, rolled it into a ball, thrown it to the ground and jumped up and down on it. Meenakshi took it from her and smoothed it out.

'Varo wants to see me to discuss topics for the essays I need to write? Why didn't he just tell you?'

'Why doesn't he discuss them with you in your next lesson? He probably wants to murder you, like he murdered Kras.'

'You sound like Kalban. Nobody's trying to murder me. I'm leaving Melucha soon anyway.'

'Foreign visitors are *supposed* to be off-limits, but people keep trying to get into your room disguised as palace staff. *Four* different people came to collect the laundry this morning. One of them was actually *carrying* an asp. Maybe Varo wants to keep you from finding out that he's guilty.'

'Why would Varo have murdered Kras?'

'Why would he want to discuss essays so urgently? Your next class is tomorrow. Does he think you'll be sitting up outlining your research all night?'

'That's insane,' Meenakshi protested. 'He can't *do* anything to me . . . He could try, but . . . well . . . it would be like . . .'

'Like a Free Bow Initiate sneaking into the palace in Madh and getting turned into a tortoise,' Gopali said.

'Exactly!'

'This isn't Madh!'

'I can still turn him into a tortoise.'

'And cause untold trouble in the process. The writ of the Magical Activities Legislative Board doesn't run in Melucha. But that's not the point. If you don't see an attack coming, you can't defend yourself.'

'I'll be careful. But I think you're wrong about Varo.'

'Nobody here has *any* idea which side Varo is on. He's not shown support for either Kalban or Abhinav—nor, as far as I can find out, for any *other* family. He claims to protect the interests of the city.'

'That's good, isn't it?'

Gopali scoffed, but said nothing.

'But if he means–'

Meenakshi stopped short at Gopali's urgently raised hand.

'Shhh!' she hissed. 'Listen!'

Meenakshi listened. She was about to suggest that Gopali should return to Madh for some rest, since the stress of Melucha appeared to be unhinging her, when a faint sibilance came to her ears.

'This is *insupportable*!' Gopali strode to the desk and threw it open.

Curled in a heap atop of a stack of writing paper was a snake with scales of a mottled grey and green pattern. It opened its mouth, flicking a forked tongue between its fangs.

'Fetch a basket!' Gopali snapped. 'In the corner by the window.'

Meenakshi had never heard that tone in her voice before. Not wanting to argue with it, she went to the corner Gopali had indicated and brought one of the wickerwork baskets stacked there.

Gopali, displaying an ability Meenakshi had never suspected she possessed, scooped the snake into the basket with her hands and slammed the lid down. She fastened the hasp and left it in the corridor.

'Do you think Varo left it here when he came?' asked Meenakshi.

'He couldn't have done. I didn't leave him alone for a moment. But if he did . . .' She trailed off. Meenakshi almost felt sorry for Varo if he turned out to be the originator of the snake and Gopali found out.

She glanced at Varo's note, which was still in her hand. 'Can I ask him to come here?'

Gopali looked at her, considering. It was the sort of thing that would be inconceivable at home. Nobody in Madh, not the High Priest of the Sun God, not the Governor's daughter, not the Governor himself, summoned the Master of the Academy or any of the staff to a meeting without notice.

But nobody in Madh left scorpions in people's beds, either.

'All right,' she said. 'Wait here. I'll get him.'

'Hasn't he gone home?'

'He's elected to stay in the palace as long as we're here.'

Left alone, Meenakshi opened the top book in the stack Varo had left for her. It began with three chapters on the importance of institutions to the functioning of society. She would have to get him to find another. No reasonable person could ask her to plod through this.

She closed the book and pushed it away. She wished her uncle hadn't insisted on sending her here. He could have persuaded a tutor from Melucha—perhaps Varo himself—to come to Madh for a few months. Most scholars were delighted to spend that length of time at the Academy, which, in addition to providing visiting professors with the opportunity to share their knowledge with a host of eager minds, paid very well.

She hadn't long to wait. Perhaps Varo had been expecting her to ask to see him.

'Meenakshi,' he said. 'I trust you've had a productive day? I heard you and Kalban had been out with . . . Chitralekha, is it? I can't imagine Rati was pleased to be investigated.'

'Is anyone pleased to be investigated?'

'Perhaps not. But that's not why we're here. I want to discuss your evaluation. Your uncle tells me the Royal Academy in Madh won't accept my word that you've learnt Political Science. They need evidence. I have no experience in setting exams and I wouldn't know how to begin marking them, especially with only one student. I thought it might suit us both if you wrote essays instead.'

'Essays,' Meenakshi repeated. Essays were worse than exams.

'Given the practical use to which you, in particular, will one day be required to put this subject, your essays should focus on the applications of the theories you will read about in the books I have prescribed.'

Meenakshi was assailed by a sudden suspicion.

'Have *you* read those books?'

'I must confess that I have not. I was not fortunate enough to have the sort of education that includes the study of detailed volumes of comparative politics. I have been assured by several people who *have* read them that they are very useful.'

'Were those people your enemies?'

'Why don't you try *one* book and see how you get on? In the meantime, there's a Privy Council meeting tomorrow. I want you to attend it.'

'Will the Privy Council allow it?' Gopali asked. 'She's a foreigner.'

'This isn't a closed meeting. Any citizen of Melucha can observe it from the gallery. I see no reason for anyone to object to Meenakshi's doing the same. Foreign observers aren't unheard of. While tomorrow's meeting is about scorpion breeding regulations—a rather dreary subject for an outsider—I want you to pay particular attention to the members of the Privy Council. Later we will discuss what you have learnt about them from your observations during the meeting.'

Meenakshi suppressed a groan. This must have been what Kalban felt like when the Chair of Mathematics made him study Theory of Numbers.

'Is that all?' she asked. 'Or is there another task that's going to give me years of nightmares?'

'I know you'll find it dull. Attending meetings is dull. Watching them is worse. But you will have to attend many in your career, and it's best if you can learn to put the time to good use. People reveal their characters even while discussing routine matters. It might interest you that Rati will be present tomorrow. She's been reinstated to the Privy Council.'

'Oh.'

'There's one other thing.'

'What?' Meenakshi asked. With her luck it would be one other thing that was drearier than listening to Councillors drone about regulations.

'Kras's wife wants to speak to you. Alone.'

Yes, worse than the Privy Council.

'*Why?*'

'Perhaps she has information about who might have killed her husband, and she's reluctant to give it to Kalban or Chitralekha.'

'I'm sure she'd prefer to talk to Kalban. Everyone does.' Meenakshi looked at Gopali for help. 'Doesn't everyone always prefer to talk to Kalban?'

'It's true,' Gopali agreed. 'And, if I might be honest, a woman who's been recently bereaved shouldn't be subjected to Meenakshi.'

'Normally I would defer to your judgement in the matter. But, although it was many years ago, Angana's family was in direct opposition to the Prince. Her reluctance to speak to Kalban isn't unreasonable.'

'Let her speak to Chitralekha. There can't be any objection to that.'

'I'm quite certain she's never met a Celestial Dancer in the entire course of her existence. She would prefer to speak to a mortal. I'll bring her to our lesson tomorrow afternoon. Consider it part of the course. Oh, and it would be as well not to mention this to Kalban or Chitralekha. They might think it their duty to question poor Angana and she ought to be spared that sort of unpleasantness.'

Without waiting to listen to any of the arguments Meenakshi was marshalling to her cause, he left the room.

'You're right,' Meenakshi said to Gopali, now equalling her gloom. 'We need to get back to Madh as soon as possible. Magical mishaps I can deal with. Everyone here expects me to *talk* to people I don't know.'

'I agree, this is odd. And what's odder is that—'

There was a knock at the door.

'Does everyone in Melucha go visiting after dinner?' Meenakshi muttered, as Gopali went to see who it was.

Meenakshi heard hushed, urgent conversation. Then Gopali led in a figure wearing a dark cloak and hood.

Meenakshi brightened. She was accustomed to cloaked and hooded people. They formed part of the landscape of Madh. They tended to impart important information and disappear into the night, with no expectation of pleasantries.

'My name isn't important,' said the cloaked individual, in the raspy whisper of a disguised voice, and with total disregard for the fact that Meenakshi, who knew how this worked, hadn't expressed any curiosity about his name. 'I have information that I can no longer keep secret. I can't trust anyone in the Prince's family. *You* will do the right thing.'

'What information do you have?'

'I know who poisoned the tutor's tea.'

'You do?' Meenakshi wasn't surprised. Why else would he have come? 'How?'

'I was there when he bought the hemlock. He didn't see me. It was late. He went to the large shop in the Tradesmen's Quarter, not to a specialist apothecary. *That* was suspicious. Normally he patronizes the big poison purveyor in the Old Town, like the other nobles. If he didn't go there, it was because he didn't want to be recognized. It was the night *before*.'

'The night before Kras was killed?'

'*Yes*,' said the voice, a hint of exasperation cutting through the rasp. 'Which other night could I mean? I saw him buy the hemlock. He said he had a special use for it.'

'Whom did you see?'

'The younger prince. Abhinav.'

'You saw Abhinav?' Meenakshi didn't know whether she should have expected that. Kalban would. 'Where were you?'

'I can't tell you more. I won't put myself in danger. You have the important facts now. Goodbye.'

The figure rose and fled through the door.

Meenakshi stared at Gopali.

'Do you think anyone else will come knocking?'

'There's no need to take the chance. Go to bed.'

CHAPTER X

The first time Kalban saw Meenakshi the following morning was when she slipped into the gallery and settled into a seat in the shadow of a convenient pillar.

He stifled a chuckle. If she hoped to avoid Varo's observation and daydream instead of taking notes, she was going to be disappointed. Varo might not be much of a scholar, but when it came to spotting people concealed behind bits of masonry, he had no equal. Meenakshi, never having attended regular classes at the Academy, had never learnt how to doze off while looking like she was enrapt by the discussion.

The herald announced his father, bringing the group around the long table to its feet with many scrapings and rustlings. The Prince of Melucha waited for his titles to be read, entered the room and took the time to fix every attendee with his intense gaze. More than one person fidgeted.

'Thank you for coming,' he said, taking his chair. It was the signal for everyone else to sit, with far less noise than they'd made while rising. 'As you may have noticed, we have an observer from Madh in the gallery this morning. I have given my permission. Order of business, please?'

Varo rose and began to read.

Kalban spent the next two hours making pertinent remarks about safety regulations (after all, no breeder wanted the scorpions to escape and sting people unintentionally when there were always parties willing to pay good money to make it happen on purpose) while trying at the same time to see who looked like taking his side for the succession and who was planning to put a few of the scorpions (bred according to the soon-to-be-updated guidelines of the Venomous Animal Husbandry Regulations) in his bed.

When there was a recess, Kalban glanced at the gallery again. He was unsurprised to find that Meenakshi wasn't paying the slightest attention.

He looked around and met Rati's eye. She was sitting a little further down the long table, on the opposite side. She smiled at Kalban with no friendliness. 'I suppose we should at least be grateful it hasn't started to rain inside the chamber.'

Kalban sighed and sat back. He ought to be using the recess to speak to people. That was the point of the Privy Council. One didn't gather the most powerful people in the city to discuss whether enchanted escape-proof cages should be imported from Madh. This was his chance to lay the groundwork for his own cause in the inevitable disputes over the succession—groundwork that was very much needed, judging by the fact that Abhinav was the centre of a bustling group of people, while he himself sat in solitary state with his order paper for company.

How much did the succession matter? If he was ousted and exiled from Melucha, he could always return to Madh and assist Paras, and later Meenakshi, with the mundane aspects of administration that, according to Asamanjas, every Governor of Madh had ignored.

But Kalban could only go to Madh if he avoided death-by-venomous-reptile in the meantime.

He was about to go and say something to Rati—one had to start somewhere and she *had* smiled, even if she had done it like a man-eating tiger laying its eyes on a likely-looking woodcutter—when he caught sight of Amar the court bard sitting in his chair near the door.

In considering who might have killed Kras, he'd never given any thought to Amar. Court bards weren't part of the web of politics. They played an instrument of their choice and sang overdone banalities about moons and lilies. They didn't kill people.

Neither did tutors. Things had changed in the years he'd been away.

Kalban leaned across the table to make an idle remark about the weather to the Prince's Treasurer, keeping an eye on Amar as he did.

Amar was listening as avidly as Varo probably thought Meenakshi should. He had to, of course. One couldn't be inoffensively entertaining unless one knew with a high degree of certainty what would offend people. Still . . . who better than Amar to be a useful participant in a plot? Full of information and unlikely to be suspected.

Kalban continued to engage the Treasurer on the subject of whether it was likely to rain, what impact that would have on the wheat and whether it would be necessary to dip into the public coffers to supply the people with bread. This had not been done in living memory.

Pür, thanks to the willingness of the Maharaja to allow magicians to make discreet interventions when necessary, usually had a surplus crop. The Maharaja was always willing to trade with Melucha. His father, the late Maharaja, had, through the judicious use of poisons, daggers and pits of vipers, gone from thirty-eighth in line to the ultimate prize of the throne. The present Maharaja was mindful that the idea that had occurred to one person might occur to others who shared the misfortune of wanting the throne while standing several lateral lines away from it. Therefore, he always liked to have an ample stock of the latest in sharp, heavy and venomous deterrents to sedition.

However, discussion of the likelihood of having to supply the citizenry out of the Prince's funds was a common way of ascertaining where other members of the aristocracy stood on matters such as poor people having bread. Most of them took the practical view that, since starving peasants were peasants who might decide to storm the high gates of the mansions of the Old Town and murder their aristocratic inhabitants, money spent on keeping them well fed was a worthwhile expense.

After a stilted conversation, in which Rati and the Chief Marshal also took part, the session resumed. Several people had strong views on scorpion breeding (that it was an ancient tradition and should be respected) and were unconcerned by the possibility of accidents (if you were silly enough to be stung by a scorpion that hadn't been left in your slipper intentionally, you deserved it). It was another hour before the session was adjourned and Kalban could go see if Meenakshi had heard a word of the debate.

Chitralekha joined them. She had been waiting outside. While Meenakshi, as a foreigner and a magician but still a mortal, might be tolerated in the gallery during the Privy Council meeting, a Celestial Dancer would not.

'I can see a lot has happened,' Kalban said. Meenakshi had the expression that meant she was planning to start at the chronological beginning of events and go through them with meticulous attention to detail and none to urgency. 'Tell me the thing you think will interest me the most.'

'Someone came to my room last night and said he saw Abhinav buying hemlock the day before Kras died.'

'That'll do it,' Chitralekha muttered, as Kalban searched for words.

'That makes no sense,' he said at last.

'That was not what I expected you to say,' said Meenakshi. 'Why doesn't it make sense? *You* think Abhinav's guilty.'

'I think he might be. I'm not saying he *wouldn't* have murdered Kras, but being *seen* buying hemlock the very day before he was poisoned? No such luck. He can't be that stupid.'

'Why don't we ask him?' Meenakshi suggested.

Kalban groaned. 'You *would* say something like that. We don't come out and *ask* people things, especially not things like, "Did you murder your old tutor?"'

'He must know that you suspect him! Have you got a better idea?'

'I'm sorry.' Abhinav appeared at Kalban's shoulder. 'Am I interrupting something?'

'Hasn't anyone taught you it's bad manners to sneak up on people?' Kalban barked.

'No. Hasn't anyone ever taught you it's stupid to hold a private conversation with your *back* to a room full of people? Don't worry, though. I'm not offended.'

'Offended?'

'That you suspect me of having murdered Kras on no stronger grounds than that *someone* told Meenakshi I was buying hemlock in the Tradesmen's Quarter the day before Kras died.'

'I never said it was the Tradesmen's Quarter,' Meenakshi said, narrowing her eyes.

'You didn't have to. I know where I bought hemlock.'

'So you *admit* it?'

'Admit that I bought hemlock? Why would I deny it? It's legal to possess hemlock in Melucha. But I *didn't* murder Kras. The purchase of hemlock goes none of the way towards showing that I did.'

'Then why,' asked Chitralekha, 'did you buy it the day before Kras died?'

'Ask to see the shop records. You'll find that dozens of people bought hemlock the day before Kras died. I don't suppose you're accusing them *all* of murdering him.'

'They weren't all at dinner with him.'

'That, I admit, was an unhappy coincidence. In any case, I don't see why you care. As I understood it, you're only here because the lady in charge–'

'Rambha,' Chitralekha specified.

'*Rambha* is concerned that either Kalban or my mother might have killed Kras as a prelude to greater and more magical acts of evil. I can tell you it's unlikely that Mother did. She prefers to stay out of politics. I don't suppose Kalban did, either. He seemed to think Kras could teach Meenakshi something worthwhile.'

'I can't take your word for that.'

'Of course you can't. That wasn't the point. If you're here because you need to make certain nobody with magical power has turned murderous, I don't see why you're concerned about who *did* kill Kras. You need to know that Kalban and my mother *didn't* kill him. Take my advice, go into both their alibis in as much detail as you want, eliminate them, and go back to the Inter-Realm.'

Chitralekha's gaze darkened to a gimlet gleam that reminded Kalban that she was Immortal. 'Are you *threatening* me?'

'I shouldn't dream of it,' Abhinav said. 'I'm advising you against wasting your time. It makes no difference to me. If anything, I'd prefer that we *did* find the truth. We've become too careless with murder in Melucha. But very few people feel as I do. Or, at best, they agree that it *is* a problem but think it's *our* problem. If it hadn't been for Kalban's return, I doubt you would be here.'

Abhinav laughed, gave Chitralekha a friendly nod and went on his way. Before he could leave the room, Rati drew him aside.

Kalban watched them go back to the table.

'Kalban,' said Chitralekha, 'this is one battle you won't win.'

'We'll see about that,' said Kalban grimly. 'It's not happened yet.'

'Abhinav's wrong about one thing. I want to find out who did it, even if it wasn't you or your mother.'

'Why?'

'The Sprites. They're always telling us we can't do what they can, because they know more about mortal psychology. If I go back without the name of the murderer, they'll be all over us—and Rambha *hates* it when they get the upper hand. She'll demote me all the way down to Probationer. It'll take centuries to work my way up again. I need to find out.'

'Have *you* got any new information?'

'What new information could I get?' Chitralekha said. 'The magical output readings won't do us any good. I'm not allowed to *talk* to anyone. I was hoping one of you would have something—'

She was interrupted by a sonorous gong.

'Lunchtime,' Kalban announced. 'Lunch in the main dining hall on Privy Council days, so Meenakshi might get away with pretending to be mute. And she has Varo after that. Suppose we meet tomorrow morning and compare notes? We'll see how far we've come.'

CHAPTER XI

With Abhinav's unexpected appearance, and then being hustled off to lunch, where her attempts to find a place in a quiet corner of the table were foiled by two members of the Privy Council who sat on either side of her to question her about her father's policies on Inter-Realm relations, Meenakshi forgot about Varo's visit the previous night.

When she entered his room to find a woman waiting with him, she was too startled to respond to his greeting.

From the fact that she was wearing the pale grey of Meluchan mourning, Meenakshi concluded that the woman must be Angana.

She stopped short in the doorway, wishing she'd remembered in time to claim to be too ill to come to class.

She could open a portal back to Madh from the schoolroom. There would be trouble, and the Portals Regulation Authority would send her a notice, but that could be dealt with. Her uncle's reaction would be harder to contain, but she could manage—

'Wait,' said the woman, before Meenakshi could put her plan into action. 'I want to talk, that's all. I promise I won't make it uncomfortable,' she added.

Meenakshi paused, looking at her closely. Although she was wan, with dark circles around her eyes, she seemed composed.

'My name is Angana,' the woman went on. 'And you must be Meenakshi.'

'Yes.'

'Paras's daughter—yes, I've met your father. He was here for the Prince's wedding. Everyone was. The Maharaja of Pür—the High Lord of Vraja—but you're not here to listen to me reminisce.'

'I was here for a lesson,' Meenakshi said. 'I can come back at a better time. I'm sure you want to talk to Varo about . . . things. Don't let me interrupt you.'

'I want to talk to *you*. Please, sit down.'

Unable to think of an excuse, Meenakshi sank into the nearest chair, piling her books on her knees. She was glad now that Varo had supplied so many of them. They made a useful barrier between her and whatever was about to happen.

'I want to talk,' Angana repeated. 'Everyone is afraid I'll go to pieces, but I was raised better than that.'

'I don't understand why you want to talk to me,' Meenakshi said. 'There's nothing I can do to help you. I didn't know your husband, I don't know anyone in Melucha except Kalban—'

'That is precisely why you can help me.'

'I don't understand,' Meenakshi said again, trying to conceal her frustration.

She wasn't *used* to not understanding. She dealt in sensible things, like Mathematics and Alchemy and the Principles of Literature. They were logical. People? She didn't understand people. She didn't *want* to understand people. That was why she didn't deal with people. That was what Kalban was for.

'Kras is dead. It was unexpected, but it wasn't a shock. I like to think I'm practical. It wasn't the first time I've lost someone close to me, and Kras was many years older than I am. I knew it was likely that I would outlive him. I have my own work. I'll survive. I'm not . . . *lost*. He was in reasonably good health, but we were prepared.'

'Then–'

'Kras was murdered,' Angana said. 'That I can't abide.'

'I thought–in Melucha–'

'People murder people in Melucha. It's part of the game. But there are rules. You can't murder *anyone*. That would be anarchy, not statecraft. Those who have power or seek it, those who join in the politics at the heart of our great city, do so at the risk of their lives–and they *know* it. They're prepared for it. It's not meant to touch anyone *else*.'

She paused, glanced at Varo and chose a chair near enough to be in Meenakshi's direct line of vision without crowding her.

'Do you think the city could run if it were otherwise? To everyone in Melucha who isn't part of the traditional quest for power–from those farming the lands surrounding the city to those running the mansions in the Old Town or the shops in the Tradesmen's Quarter–life is *normal. Safe.* People like Kras, who aren't a threat to anyone, aren't meant to be affected by anything that happens in the palace, except perhaps a loss of patronage when there's a change in government.' Angana shrugged. 'That's a risk of doing business anywhere.'

'Are you sure?' Meenakshi couldn't help asking.

'Sure?'

'Are you sure your husband wasn't doing anything that might have put him in danger?'

'Did someone tell you he was? Rati? Or perhaps Kalban? There have always been rumours. There are bound to be, in a place like Melucha. You can't believe everything you hear.'

'I thought he was expelled from his position as Abhinav's tutor.'

'That was his guilelessness rather than the opposite. Rati confused him. She's so . . . so *forceful*, and Kras isn't—*wasn't*—accustomed to court life. We were sure Kalban had no intention of returning from Madh. Why should he? By all accounts, he was happy there, and had the free use of his magical power.'

'That doesn't explain why Kras gave Rati information about Abhinav.'

'Rati persuaded him that since Kalban wasn't returning, it was Kras's responsibility to train Abhinav for his future role. She said she wanted to *help* him—so she could be certain, *everyone* could be certain he was ready. I agree it's flimsy reasoning, but Kras—how do I explain it? He was a scholar at heart. It would never occur to him that Rati had her own ends, and if it did he would never imagine that her ends were anything other than the greater good of Melucha.'

'There might be many ways of defining the greater good of Melucha.'

'Perhaps. The rumours about Kras started again when Kalban returned a few months ago. I know they were false. Kras knew I had already lost my parents and my brother.'

'They were banished, not killed. Why didn't you go with them if it mattered that much to you?'

'Why didn't I go with them?' Angana considered the question. 'I was very young and did as I was told. My parents thought I would be safe in Melucha. They weren't wrong. We don't bear grudges; nobody has held their actions against me. But I lost my position, I lost everything I knew. It was difficult. Kras wouldn't have put me through that again. That Kalban wanted Kras to tutor you should be proof enough for you that Kras never plotted against him. You have no reason to trust me, but Kalban wouldn't have suggested Kras for you if he'd imagined any trouble.'

'I still don't know what you want me to do.'

'I want you to give me justice. You're the only one who might do it. The Celestial Dancer won't care about anything other than her mission. If it *isn't* Kalban or Persis who murdered Kras, it's of small importance to anyone from the Inter-Realm. Kalban . . . he's your friend. I won't speak against him. He's a nice boy, but he's too closely involved. You're not one of us. You have nothing to gain in Melucha. Although I've heard you don't particularly care for people, I've met your parents—both of them—and I'm sure any daughter of theirs must care for truth.'

'I don't know—'

'I want you to give me justice. I won't lie—I think I know who murdered my husband. Proof is another matter. You're the only one who might get it.'

'Is there anything *you* can tell me?' Meenakshi asked. 'You must know better than anybody if he had any enemies, and who might have wanted to kill him.'

'If you want my opinion, it must have been Rati. She tried to use Kras for her plots. She failed, but maybe she thought Kras knew more than he did. She might have been afraid of what he would tell you—or tell Kalban. Kras was always fond of Kalban.'

'Everyone's pointing the finger at someone else,' Meenakshi murmured. 'I don't see—this isn't like a problem in Mathematics or a conundrum in Philosophy.'

'I think you'll find that it's a little like both. I *have* faith in you,' Angana said. 'You must not fail me.'

Meenakshi didn't have to go looking for Kalban after the lesson. He was waiting outside the door. As soon as she emerged, he pulled her into the room opposite, which was also arranged like a schoolroom.

'Yes, this was the one we used for our early education,' Kalban said, in response to Meenakshi's questioning look.

Glancing around, Meenakshi spotted a copy of *A for Assassin* in the bookshelf and an array of daggers in a glass case by the window. There was a display of poisonous herbs, each carefully labelled in a childish scrawl, in another case.

'Did you learn *any* normal things?' Meenakshi asked. 'Or was it all how to murder?'

'How *not* to be murdered,' Kalban corrected. 'Nobody teaches how to murder. People learn that on their own. And to answer your question, yes, we learnt all the non-magical subjects.'

'You didn't learn magic?'

'My mother taught me a little. There aren't any tutors for magic in Melucha.'

'How do people learn magic if they can't go to Madh?'

'If they don't have a family member who can help, they teach themselves, which causes a lot of unpleasant accidents. That's part of the reason magic has such a bad reputation in Melucha. It's a vicious cycle. But that wasn't what I wanted to talk to you about. What happened with Varo?'

'You mean the essays?'

'I mean with Angana. Did she come to meet you?'

'Oh, Gopali told you.' Meenakshi brightened. 'There wasn't time this morning. Yes, she came. She wasn't what I expected.'

'Most people aren't what *you* expect. We don't need to be concerned about that, particularly in the case of a grieving widow.'

'No, that's not what I mean. She seemed . . . self-possessed. Gopali thought I might upset her. She warned Varo. But Angana didn't seem like she intended to be upset. She . . . I suppose she's sad,' Meenakshi said. 'It was more like . . .'

'Take your time,' said Kalban. There was no point rushing Meenakshi when it came to unravelling people's motives. He was lucky she was trying at all.

'She wasn't sad,' Meenakshi said at last. 'She was *offended*. I think the murder offended her sense of . . . of rightness.

She didn't *want* Kras to die, of course, but she said he was much older . . .'

She paused to look at Kalban questioningly.

'He was,' Kalban confirmed. 'He'd been the Royal Tutor for a very long time, and seen several transitions of power without getting involved. That's why I was so surprised he got himself expelled.'

'Maybe she was right. Angana said,' Meenakshi explained, 'that Kras wasn't knowingly involved in any plots. She said Rati tricked him—somehow—and Kras didn't have the experience to see through her.'

'*That* I find difficult to believe. Kras had been at court since he was a young man. He had decades on Rati. He was no fool . . . But neither is Rati, so maybe she did trick him.'

'Rati said he was involved in the plot to overthrow your father.'

'She might have lied.'

'Why should she?'

'Because if it's true that she tricked Kras, that he *wasn't* a part of her plot, she had a motive to kill him. As long as he was pensioned off and in disgrace, he was no threat to her. If he came into favour again, and especially if he lived at the palace and had the opportunity of meeting everyone, there was the danger that he'd talk. I'm sure there were things that didn't come out at the time. She must have had backup plans. It wouldn't matter, but if she's been trying to get back in . . .' Kalban waved a hand. '*In* everything, she won't want people to know.'

'That's what Angana said. But it doesn't explain why she should lie about his part in the earlier plot.'

'That makes it seem like Kras had been scheming with one person or another for years. If *that* were true, there would be more people with a motive to kill him than just Rati.'

'I want to go out,' Meenakshi said. 'There's an oppressive atmosphere in here.'

'Yes. It would be nice to get some fresh air. Let's go to the Tradesmen's Quarter. We can interview the man who sold Abhinav the hemlock. You remember the name on the bill of purchase?'

'Yes, but what's the point of that? Abhinav admitted he bought it.'

'He did, but something strikes me as odd about this situation. The sort of person who loiters around an apothecary in the Tradesmen's Quarter isn't the sort who'd be able to sneak into the palace to give you anonymous information. Maybe we'll learn something. Get yourself a cloak, it's going to be a chilly evening.'

The Tradesmen's Quarter was very different from the Old Town.

At first, it was just that the houses were smaller, the high walls and vast front lawns giving way to low fences behind which narrow strips of dirt or mosaic tiling stood between the houses and the road.

Then they'd turned on to *another* road, and this one looked exactly like it housed purveyors of poisons. The uneven cobbles made the coach rattle and jolt—'So nobody can sneak up unannounced,' Kalban told her—and the dingy buildings crowded close on either side. There were no fences or gardens.

A covered channel on one side of the road emitted a bubbling sound that would have been normal in any Alchemy lab.

'Don't go near it,' Kalban said, when Meenakshi leaned out the window to look. 'It's the runoff from poison making.'

'They don't sell hemlock in leaf form?'

'They do, but they also distil poisons into tiny vials—the sort you can conceal in a ring or a bracelet.'

Meenakshi had noticed that people in Melucha wore a lot of jewellery.

The carriage stopped outside a shop that looked a little less disreputable than the others on the street. The large windows showed off locked cases containing an array of gold and silver ornaments on one side, and gem-inlaid boxes on the other.

A bell above the door rang when Kalban pushed it open.

Meenakshi followed him in, looking around in fascination. Huge jars stood in rows on one wall. They had labels like *Datura, 2* and *Foxglove, 3.5*. A table nearby held an array of what looked like wands, but when she reached out to examine one, Kalban pulled her back and showed her the tiny button that, when pressed, caused a wicked-looking blade to spring glinting out of each end.

There was one other customer, negotiating the sale of an intricate set of goblets. The clerk at the counter was exquisitely dressed in bright colours. He had nothing of the sinister air that someone selling the means of death to the general public should exude.

'You'll note that it's a slow release mechanism,' the clerk was saying to the customer, who was wrapped in a thick cape and hood. He was several inches taller than Kalban, and broad in the shoulder, so he was probably a man. 'You want to serve a fine, aged wine, that your guest will savour. Preferably something strong, or spiced, to encourage him to take his time and mask the taste.'

'I'll do the talking,' Kalban said, as the customer began counting out coins from a velvet pouch. 'You stand here and don't touch *anything*.'

The clerk nodded to them as he wrapped up the goblets.

The customer took them and strode out. Kalban turned to look after him.

'The Treasurer's secretary, if I'm not wrong,' he murmured. 'I wonder what *he's* planning. I should tell my father not to accept any invitations until we know.'

'May I help you?' said the clerk, coming into the centre of the room. 'I have a wide array of jewellery that might interest the lady. This piece in particular . . .' Unlocking a case, he took out a complicated array of gold chains and rings. 'You'll note that it has three separate slots for vials and one that can hold a fine powder. They can each—or all, together—be released with a casual gesture. It is both beautiful and efficient.'

'No, thank you,' Kalban said. 'We want to buy hemlock. I need to replenish my stores.'

'Of course,' said the clerk, leading the way to the jars. 'Now *this* is an excellent vintage, about three years old. The crop that year was potent.'

'Is it a popular variety?'

'It is much favoured by people of discernment. Naturally there's . . . er . . . a small, a *very* minor surcharge, which, when you've tried it, you'll agree is justified considering the effectiveness. Death is almost instantaneous.'

'I would prefer something whose action is not quite so immediate.'

'Ah, you'd like to be far away when it happens. In that case, might I recommend *this*?' The man took down a jar, unwrapped the string holding the heavy cloth sealing it shut and tilted it towards Kalban. 'You'll notice that it has no odour. Of course, a greater amount is required in order for the poison to take effect. This is best for adding to mildly flavoured dishes, but it must be used in large quantities.'

'Have you sold much of this recently?'

'Sales of hemlock have been slow. I believe it was last week that I made my last sale, and nothing before that for almost a fortnight. I find that many of my customers now prefer Datura. Perhaps I could interest you in that?' He ran his hand along the jars. 'I have a sample here that came in last week from Vraja—expensive, of course.' He shook his head. 'It's very difficult to get foreign poisons these days. For some reason, governments are trying to clamp down on their export. I can give you enough for one use at half-price, and I can order more if you find you like it.'

'No, I'll just have the hemlock. Which one did you sell last week?'

The clerk shot Kalban a sharp glance, but his tone of easy complaisance didn't change. 'I'm afraid I'm out of that. I don't think you'll find it useful for your purposes anyway.'

'No?'

'No, it was the last remnant of a remarkably fast-acting crop. My personal belief is that it was a hybrid—the leaves didn't look like pure hemlock, as you would have known if you'd had the opportunity to see them.'

'A hybrid with what?'

'I wish I knew. The grower wouldn't give away her secrets—and who can blame her? It caused death within seconds. Now, can I interest you in *this* stock?' He took down another jar. 'It came in this morning. It's from a farm that's always given me excellent results.'

'Slow?'

'Slow to normal. Do you want something very slow? Then the one I suggested earlier would be best.'

'I'll take that, thank you.'

'Would you also like a dagger?' Quicker than the eye could see, he whipped one from his sleeve. 'This is a particularly elegant design. There's an ingenious mechanism that sends poison from a hidden vial down ridges in the blade when the ruby on the hilt is touched. The merest scrape is enough. It entirely eliminates uncouth stabbing at the heart.'

'The hemlock,' Kalban said. 'Thank you.'

CHAPTER XII

Meenakshi was shaken awake while the sky visible through the window was still littered with stars.

'*What?*' she muttered, assuming it was Gopali who'd come to complain about someone having blown poison darts through her bedroom window. Still half asleep, she waved a hand in the general direction of the lamp, which flared to life.

It was Chitralekha.

'*What?*' Meenakshi asked, more irritably.

'I wanted to talk to you alone.'

'And you couldn't have done that at a normal time?'

'This place is a beehive,' Chitralekha said. 'There are always people polishing the statues and carrying jugs of wine around and *watching*. I'm certain Persis is having me followed. I've had an idea. Do you think it was Kras doing the scorpion breeding?'

'You woke me two hours early to talk about scorpion breeding? You may not need sleep, but I do!'

'This is important.'

'It's also important to be well rested. Father told me that once he tried a four-point time modification to a basic cleansing spell when he'd only slept three hours the night before, and—'

'Ah, yes, I remember hearing about that. Wasn't that when he was trying to improve the statuary along the merchants' pier in Madh? The carvings were in a dreadful condition, I agree. They were covered with moss and lichen—'

'And the lions came to life and chased someone all the way back to the Academy.'

'It was, in fact, the present Master of the Academy,' Chitralekha said, eyes twinkling. 'He and your father have always had their problems.'

'See? We don't want one of the Maidens with Water Pots coming to life and . . . pouring water on someone? I'm not sure what they'd do.'

'These statues are polished everyday. That's the reason it's so hard to have a private conference. You don't need to scrape lichen off them, with or without magic. Now stop arguing and listen to me. I thought young students were supposed to keep late hours.'

'Not when they have to spend all day talking to strangers.'

'It's good practice for you. As I said, it occurs to me that Kras is the likeliest candidate. Think about it. It must be someone who had constant access to the palace, which rules out Rati and Dev—'

'Rati and Dev? What have they got to do with this?'

'I thought it might be connected to Kras's murder.'

'There's no proof of that.'

'We'll put that aside for now. The people who have daily access to the Lotus, which would have been necessary while the breeding was active and required supervision, are Shel, Persis and Abhinav, the members of the Privy Council, and the palace staff, whom I think we can eliminate.'

'That's a lot of people.'

'We have more to go on. The room has been abandoned for some time. Kras was expelled, which would explain it.'

'He wasn't the only one who stopped coming. Rati fell out of favour.'

'Why would Rati need to breed scorpions in a secret chamber in Kalban's bedroom? She has a good home of her own, presumably with its own secret rooms where she can breed whatever she wants. Imagine the scandal if she were caught in the private family quarters of the Lotus. No, Kras is the perfect choice. As long as he was Abhinav's tutor, he could explain himself if he *did* get caught.'

'That doesn't explain why Kras would want to breed scorpions.'

'Money, I expect. There's a lot of it in the scorpion breeding trade. I looked into the tax records while you and Kalban went shopping yesterday. It's a huge business. That's why they want to regulate it. If you'd paid attention to any of the books Kalban has given you on the subject, you'd know most scorpions don't have enough venom to kill an adult. Of course there's a market for . . . modification.'

'I can imagine that, but why would it have to be secret? Kalban said it isn't illegal. And he thought it was Abhinav–'

'Kalban wants to find a way to pin this on Abhinav. Kalban *knows* most people here think Abhinav is a better choice to be ruler. Most of the Privy Council supports Kalban *officially*, but that's because they *have* to support primogeniture given their own histories. But they don't think he's inherited his parents' talents. If they could eliminate him without too much fuss, they would do it.'

'Abhinav can't do any magic—'

'No, he's exactly like his father. They can understand *that*. Kalban isn't as much of a politician as Abhinav, though I'm sure you can't tell the difference. And although he's a capable sorcerer, he doesn't have his mother's power.'

'That's no reason for Kalban to falsely accuse Abhinav of breeding scorpions.'

'I didn't say Kalban's lying. He believes what he wants to believe. Besides, if it were Abhinav, why would he leave the evidence for us to find? Breeding scorpions might be legal, but Kalban might be expected to take issue with its having been done in a secret chamber off his bedroom. But if it were Kras, he was expelled, and wouldn't have been allowed into the Lotus again, so he had no opportunity to clean up after himself.'

'What *are* you saying? Kras bred scorpions in secret, knew he'd get found out once Kalban came back, and *waited* for some months doing nothing about it while, through great good fortune, Kalban didn't discover the hidden room. Then, when he was called to the palace and had an opportunity to remove the evidence, he decided to commit suicide?'

'No. That's just it. Kras did it, and couldn't remove the evidence. I can't go past that.'

'Then maybe, as I said in the beginning, it has nothing to do with the murder. Can I go back to sleep now?'

'Maybe Kras had an accomplice. Scorpion breeding wasn't illegal, but it might have jeopardized his position. That might have been enough motive to—where are you going?'

'To get Kalban,' Meenakshi said, wrapping herself in a robe. 'If I have to do this before the crack of dawn, all to clear his name, I don't see why *he* should get to sleep. And then I'll go see if there's really boiling water in the kitchen and have a cup of tea.'

'I'll get the tea. You get Kalban—and check your slippers!' Chitralekha added, as Meenakshi started to put them on. 'I don't want Gopali to murder *me*.'

Fifteen minutes later, sitting around the table in her room with Chitralekha, Kalban and a large pot of some light invigorating tea that Chitralekha had acquired from the kitchen, Meenakshi felt considerably more cheerful, if no nearer the truth.

'We're not asking the right questions,' said Kalban, 'or looking at the right people. We've been obsessed with Rati and Dev—'

'And Abhinav,' added Chitralekha, a trifle maliciously.

'He's a logical suspect,' said Kalban, unblushing. 'But if the clerk was telling the truth, the hemlock he bought was the wrong variety, so that lets him out. Anyway we've already discussed him. We've *not* talked about Amar.'

'What reason could the court bard have for wanting to kill the Royal Tutor?'

'He's on Abhinav's side,' Kalban began.

Chitralekha groaned. 'No. *No.* See, this is the difficulty. You're unable to think about this objectively. Between you and Abhinav there are two *sides*, as you put it. Everyone has to be on one or the other and you think most people are on Abhinav's side. *Kras* was, so why would Amar kill him?'

'Kras may not have been on Abhinav's side if he was giving Rati information about him—'

'Rati is certain that he was.'

'*Fine.* Kras was plotting to put Abhinav on the throne and was expelled for behaviour unbecoming of the Royal Tutor . . . Which was what that would have been,' Kalban admitted. 'But that doesn't prove Amar's innocence. We don't know anything about him.'

'Was he here before you left?'

'He'd just begun—a few months before I left? It wasn't a full year. I didn't see all that much of him. He was at most formal banquets and he'd sing pointless songs about everyone in the room. He wasn't—he still isn't—any good.'

'Good at singing or making up poetry?'

'Neither, though that's not what I mean. A court bard isn't invited to perform at a banquet full of sworn enemies just to provide background doggerel. He's meant to know everything—everyone—and lighten the atmosphere and make people get along, if it's only for an evening. I don't know if Amar knows everyone, but he can't make people smile—or forget that they're plotting to kill the person sitting opposite.'

'I'll grant you that Amar is an angle that needs to be investigated,' said Chitralekha. 'But which of us is going to do it?'

'*How* are we to do it?' Meenakshi asked. 'Don't you people have anyone like the Counsellor here? Melucha seems like the sort of place where you could use that expertise.'

Kalban reflected on the Counsellor, who made it his business to know everything that was happening in the city of Madh. He was a terrifying man who'd once been a hired assassin, and other than the bright young spies who made up his office, Meenakshi was the only person who enjoyed his company.

'We don't because there'd be no point,' he said. 'Everyone's plotting—or spying—or double-crossing, sometimes all three at once, and sometimes in more than one direction. Everyone is on their own side. That's all you have to remember.'

'Who would know anything about Amar?'

'My mother might. She's the patron of the Association of Minstrels, Bards and Poets.'

'All right,' said Chitralekha. 'I'll talk to her. And Meenakshi can come with me. What else do we need to know? Is there anyone who was at dinner that night whom we've not considered?'

'Mada, the head of the kitchen. He'd have no reason to murder Kras. The palace staff are never under threat. They keep things running. They're far more permanent than any Prince. They'll be here no matter who rules the city.'

'Mada is alive,' said Meenakshi. 'That's a point against him.'

'What do you mean?'

'The easiest way to introduce poison into the tea would have been to put it in before it was poured, whether the murderer added it to the pot as it was being prepared or as it was waiting. Because the action was slow, Mada would have shown no ill effects, at least for as long as it took for Kras to drink the tea. Who would care about preserving the taster's life more than the taster himself?'

'Since we're on this subject,' said Chitralekha, 'we've not given serious thought to the family—other than Abhinav. The Prince has little motive. Rati was telling the truth when she said nobody wanted him deposed. But either Kalban or Persis might have done it. Don't scowl, Kalban, we have to consider every possibility.'

'Why would I kill Kras? I *wanted* him to teach Meenakshi something. I thought—I still think—that he'd have had a better shot at teaching her than Varo.'

'You might be lying about that. Let's say, *hypothetically*, that you found out Kras intended to support Abhinav's claim to the throne—'

'He had very little influence—'

'And you felt betrayed,' Chitralekha went on. 'Because he had been your childhood tutor before he was Abhinav's. You thought he was genuinely fond of you. It was a blow to find out he supported your brother. You wanted revenge, but after his expulsion Kras and his wife had moved into the suburbs. You couldn't just visit them and stab him. That might turn the Privy Council against you.'

'So I persuaded Asamanjas to send Meenakshi here so that I would have an excuse to call Kras back and murder him?' Kalban demanded, a furious flush on his face.

'I was going to say you seized the opportunity as a happy coincidence, but have it your way. You knew Kras well. You knew he never touched wine and he'd only drink his own tea. You knew the tea would conceal the smell and taste of hemlock. At some point when everyone was walking around in the library, you slipped hemlock into Kras's cup—or maybe you didn't need to put it in physically. It would have been a simple spell.'

'Check my magical output,' Kalban suggested.

'Something so minor might not register,' pointed out Meenakshi.

'Thank you. What would I do without you to help me clear my name?'

'I'm not saying you did it. I just think you should go about proving your innocence with *reason*, not outrage. The best way to do that is to find out who *did* kill Kras.'

'And *how*,' Kalban said. 'There were a lot of people and the lighting in the room is conspicuous by its lack, but it was still a risk to do it with everyone present. And about that dreadful room with the scorpions.' He glanced at Meenakshi. 'I'll need you to help me clear it out. The chambermaid will have a fit if I ask her to do it.'

'Yes, I was going to ask you about that. I was going to say we should burn it all, but now I don't think so. Where do you want to put it?'

'You were right the first time. Burn the lot.'

'Even the *books*?' Meenakshi asked in horror.

'We won't burn those,' Kalban consented. 'We can send them to your father, especially the ones about magical murder. He'll have some fun writing to their authors telling them how incompetent they are.'

Chapter XIII

Meenakshi didn't have to be cajoled into talking to Persis, whom she found comfortingly sensible in the sea of madness that was Melucha. She and Chitralekha went to her right after leaving Kalban, who had to be at another Privy Council meeting.

'Better if I'm not there anyway,' he had said, with dire foreboding. 'You're likelier to get her to answer honestly.'

Persis's study was full of familiar objects: It looked like it could have belonged to a professor at the Academy, or rather to any three professors at the Academy, each of whom was a follower of a different discipline. Meenakshi herself wasn't a proponent of the school of magical thought that believed that the most effective spells were performed in a room where large numbers of arcane objects of no discernible purpose were obscured by a fug of incense, but several people in Madh were.

Even there, Meenakshi had never seen a study that looked like its owner had ordered everything that was advertised in the classifieds of *Sorcery Monthly*.

Persis laughed when she saw Meenakshi's wide-eyed gaze rake the room.

'I know,' she said. 'It's ridiculous, isn't it? But I find it rather lonely here and this is one way of feeling a little closer to the community.'

'You used to live alone on an island.'

'I didn't have to keep up appearances on my island. It was perfect. You don't realize how much of a companion magic is until you have to spend large stretches of your days without it. I even have samples of crystal sands from each of the Mystic Isles.'

Meenakshi's attention was caught by a jade figurine of approximately feline shape.

'Is this the enchanted good luck cat? They were selling them at every street corner in Madh last year.'

'Yes, I told Kalban to get me one. I've found that the charm works in unusual ways. It doesn't bring good luck when I expect it to. But every now and then I'll find that some Privy Councillor who asked for magical activity to be punishable by imprisonment has knocked over and broken his most prized antique vase.'

Meenakshi laughed. Chitralekha, though she tried to look disapproving, couldn't hold back a smile.

'I should write you up for that,' she said. 'I won't, because I'll have to track down the people making those cats and I believe they come from the mountains north of Khand. It would take years to sort that mess out.'

'Do they have unregulated magic in Khand?' Meenakshi asked.

'After a fashion. It's small-scale. They specialize in little things, like protective amulets and good luck charms—with the occasional diversion into hex bags. People who are serious about practising magic tend to leave. In that way it's like Melucha.'

'Why did you move *to* Melucha?' Meenakshi's question was directed at Persis, who responded with a slight shrug.

'Because I was young and, to be honest, I was getting a little bored. I'd gone to live on my island with some idea of setting up a school, but nothing came of it. Parents didn't want to send their children to a deserted island with only a dangerous sorceress for chaperone. I should have thought of that.'

'A school? What *for*? If you wanted to teach, you could have stayed on at the Academy.'

'I was going through a rebellious phase. I thought I'd give people an alternative to the Academy.' Persis sighed. 'My life *would* have been different if I'd taught there . . . Anyway, my island school idea wasn't working out. The state of education in Melucha was shocking. I thought if I came to the city I could do some good, especially for students who weren't dedicated enough to go to Madh but wanted to learn *something*.'

'Did that work out?'

'As Princess Consort I have far less control over policy than I did when I was an ill-tempered sorceress living on an island far enough out to sea to be outside the reach of Melucha's territorial waters, and therefore Melucha's law. Now all I can do is argue with the Minister of Education.'

'There's a Minister of Education? I didn't see him at the Privy Council.'

'He's not important enough to be on the Privy Council,' Persis said. 'It's not a hereditary position. Officially it's awarded based on merit and held for four years. I've only ever seen Shel use it to settle minor nobles who seem to be growing discontented. The office is a solitary room in the North Wing and I believe all it does is issue an education license to anyone who can write enough to fill out the form. There's no attempt to set a standard curriculum.'

'And people don't *care*?'

'As long as it rains when it's meant to and there are no thunderstorms out of season, why worry about whether the clouds are stratus or cumulonimbus? Those who are interested enough find a way to the Academy in Madh. But,' Persis went on, 'I'm sure you're not here to discuss educational reform. What is it?'

Meenakshi glanced at Chitralekha, who gave her a slight nod. They had decided earlier that it was best to be direct with Persis, instead of trying to arrive at the issue through a roundabout route and getting nowhere but lost.

'We wanted to know about Amar,' said Meenakshi.

'Amar? The court bard? What's he been doing to you?'

'Nothing, but Kalban thought . . . We still don't know who killed Kras, and there's nothing to prove that Amar *didn't* do it. But we couldn't think of why he might have wanted to, and he thought . . . *you* might know.'

Persis looked reflective. 'I hadn't considered the possibility myself. Amar is capable of murder, I agree. Everyone is, given the right incentive.'

'What do you know about him?'

'Very little. I believe his father is a tenant farmer out on one of the estates. He never told me which estate, which makes me suspect that his family is affiliated to one of Shel's political opponents. That wouldn't have mattered to me—or to Shel. The farmers can't be held responsible when they don't have a choice in the matter.'

'Don't the farmers like their landlords?'

'That's not what I meant, although there *was* a time when that was the case. But given enough rebellions and massacres and scions of noble and ancient families being run through with pitchforks, even aristocrats will learn. They treat their tenants with fairness now, some with positive friendliness. It's worked. Most of the tenants are loyal, and wouldn't change landlords if given the opportunity.' Persis smiled. 'It's a truth conveniently ignored that most of them will never have the opportunity.'

'Kalban said Amar is on Abhinav's side.'

Persis laughed at that. 'Kalban thinks everyone is on someone else's side. You shouldn't take him too seriously when he talks like that. Amar knows Abhinav better, and most people are a little wary of Kalban's magical abilities. Those are realities he'll have to learn to deal with.'

'If Amar's father's a farmer,' said Chitralekha, 'and on a rival estate, how did he come to your attention?'

'Most landlords do their best to help their tenants, and court bard is an innocuous enough position . . . another tool to be used to settle a quarrelsome noble family. But in Amar's case, his landlord didn't recommend him to me. His predecessor was due to retire. In the months preceding the event, we were inundated with applications from every young man or woman who could identify more than two notes on a reed pipe. I didn't know, or care, who sent Amar. He was there with the rest.'

'He was the one you chose. There must have been *something* special about him.'

Persis grimaced. 'He was the best of a bad lot. There are poor pickings for the position of court bard. I tried them all out, but the others had—how shall I put it—a little *too much* ability. Someone who's a really clever poet can never be a court bard. There's artistic pride to consider. The temptation to slide in subtle ironies and try to sway public opinion with hints and double meanings will be too strong. Amar was the only one who was . . . honestly, who was such a terrible poet that he thought he'd done his bit by rhyming blue with new.'

'He doesn't get involved in politics?'

'I wouldn't go so far. He's been here for years now. I don't suppose anyone can live in the palace that long and not form some opinions. But he knows not to act on them, and he's incapable of putting them into song without being so blatant about it that I would be justified in dismissing him. He suits my purposes.'

'That doesn't help,' Meenakshi said. 'How do you get by without a Minister of Information?'

'Like the Counsellor in Madh? Most of the time we don't care. We might have the occasional murder, but, despite what Kalban must have told you, there's not an epidemic of it. The common people are untouched, so we don't have angry hordes screaming for justice.'

Meenakshi was struck by the word.

'*Justice*? That's what *she* said too—Angana,' she added, when Persis looked puzzled. 'She came to see me.'

'Meenakshi,' Chitralekha said, 'when you're investigating a murder, you don't go around revealing everything to suspects.'

'You said we weren't to call them suspects.'

'I also said you should read the books Varo gave you, and where did we go with that?'

'Varo's books are boring.'

'Maybe they are,' said Persis. 'But you'll find they're useful. Oh, you'll rule Madh without knowing how to conduct delicate negotiations, when the time comes, but it's a useful skill to have. To begin with, it'll make your life easier now.'

'Did *you* read them?'

'As a matter of fact, I did. I wasn't born in Melucha. My mother was an artist. She and my father came here when I was a girl. That was part of what attracted Shel,' she went on. 'Marrying me was better than marrying the daughter of one noble family and offending the others, because he could at least claim it was for the greater good. In any case, I knew nothing of politics, and I had been sent to Madh, to the Academy, when I was very young. As a city Madh has many virtues, but it doesn't train you to deal with court life.'

'You read them *all the way through*?'

'I did skip a few bits. The chapter on identifying poisons by symptoms was eighty-three pages long. Why would I ever need to do that? It's why there's a court physician.'

'A court physician?' Chitralekha perked up. 'Did he attend to Kras?'

'He was called to him, but don't get your hopes up. He won't be any help to you. By the time he arrived, Kras had been gone for hours. There weren't any deathbed confessions—or accusations—to help you on your way.'

'Pity,' Meenakshi said. 'That would have helped.'

'What do you have so far?'

'Nothing,' Meenakshi said. 'We've spoken to everyone—almost everyone—who was there. And everyone's telling us someone else did it, and of course it's impossible to eliminate anyone because everyone was walking around and *anyone* might have put the hemlock in Kras's cup.'

'That's how Paras would do it, too. Ask everyone what their movements were, and try to recreate the scene with a floor plan and prove that someone was lying because he said he took two steps back from the window and that would have made him collide with a bookshelf.'

'That's not a bad idea,' Meenakshi said. 'I didn't think of a floor plan.'

'That won't help you. People's memories aren't that accurate. Someone who says he stood looking a painting for a couple of minutes might mean one minute or five. A step might be two or three, or a very tiny half-step. Everyone had the opportunity to kill Kras. This being Melucha, anyone can get hemlock, and anyone can have a motive for murdering anyone else.'

'So we should give it up as a bad job?'

'Not at all. Angana had the right idea. What you're after—or, at least what you *should* be after, no matter what promotion Chitralekha is angling for—is justice, justice for the man who is dead. Maybe you need to look to *him* for answers.'

'Conjure a spirit?' Meenakshi asked, horrified. 'That's a Scale Ten violation. The Dangerous Being Control Squad would track me down here—'

'*No*,' Persis said. 'That's not what I meant. I should write to your mother about making you spend more time with people other than Paras and Asamanjas and your tutors. What you need to do, and what you ought to be able to do since Angana is willing to help you, is go through Kras's things. After the safety team was through with his room, his possessions were returned to her. Ask her to let you see them. If you want the truth, you'll find it there.'

Chapter XIV

'Tell me why we're doing this again.' Meenakshi looked up and down the corridor. 'You realize this is the sort of activity I dislike the most, sneaking around—'

'So says the person who made a flock of griffons *without* permission,' whispered Chitralekha.

'Without permission, but *openly*. When the Arcane Zoology Authorization Desk came by with their pamphlets, I didn't slink off down the corridor pretending I wasn't there.'

'The lack of this vital skill is why you've been sent here. If you'd been attending regular classes you would have learnt it. There's not a student alive who hasn't dashed into a convenient empty classroom while trying to steal undetected from a boring lesson.'

'You haven't answered my question. Why are we doing this? We don't have any proof that Amar is involved.'

'Doesn't that strike you as suspicious? There, the guards have turned the corner. Come!'

Chitralekha dashed down the corridor, managing to make no noise despite her multitude of bangles. Meenakshi followed as quietly as she could.

'Why do you wear those?' she asked Chitralekha, as she caught up with her at the door to Amar's room. 'Don't they make it harder to sneak?'

'It's locked,' Chitralekha said, trying the door. 'Open it.'

'If Kalban finds out—'

'How is it any worse than using a lock pick?'

Meenakshi tapped the padlock with one finger. It sprang open. She drew back the bolt and opened the door.

'Have you not heard the job description?' Chitralekha went on. 'I tempt powerful sorcerers away from the path of evil. Nothing tempts a mortal like an abundance of gold.'

'But you're not tempting anybody *here*. You're not allowed.'

'I'm used to them. It's part of the look. Besides, the sprites have been working on them. They've been upgraded. They're not just jewellery. Well, most of them are just jewellery, but this . . .' She touched a necklace of stones that were a little too bright to be rubies.

'Is that Chaos?' Meenakshi asked.

'No, it's the Sprites' magic that makes them so bright. I can use them to speak to headquarters. If I twist the stones in the right sequence, it opens a two-way link to the Communications Room.'

'Oh.' Meenakshi cocked her head. 'Can I look at it later?'

'You want to figure out how it works?' Chitralekha grinned. 'I'll make a deal with you. If we solve this murder, I'll let you have the necklace for a week. I'm sure you'll work it out in that time.'

Meenakshi brightened. 'What are we waiting for? Let's start searching Amar's cupboards.'

Meenakshi suited the action to the word, doing a quick sweep for magical booby traps. She didn't find any. She hadn't expected to. She unlocked the cupboards with a snap of her fingers before letting Chitralekha take the lead in opening them. A viper slithered out of the first cupboard and wrapped itself affectionately around her wrist.

'He doesn't want strangers poking around his things,' Chitralekha said, going to the window and letting the viper slink out. A few moments later, a shriek from below announced its arrival at ground level. 'Maybe he has something to hide.'

'Check the desk,' said Meenakshi. 'If there's nothing in it, I can go through his papers while you deal with the cupboards.'

Chitralekha removed a Wandering Spider from the desk and left it to Meenakshi, who began to scan the papers methodically. She passed over several half-written poems and a draft of a Jubilee Ode before she found something that looked promising.

'There's a letter,' she announced. She flipped it over to see the signature. 'From his family.' She flipped it back and looked at the address. 'They live on one of the royal estates. Persis was right.'

'The letter's standard.' Meenakshi skimmed it. 'Stay out of trouble, remember we're best off not meddling in affairs of state. Although we naturally love our own lords best—*really?*—our first loyalty must be to the ruler of Melucha . . . Do you think he copied it out of a Civics textbook?'

'Does it say that?' Chitralekha demanded.

'There's also some drivel about not succumbing to the temptations of the city.' Meenakshi turned the letter over. 'And a new type of ploughshare they're introducing to the farm.'

'Never mind the new type of ploughshare. Does it really say, "Our first loyalty must be to the ruler of Melucha"?'

'Yes. Why?'

'Meenakshi,' Chitralekha said, 'don't you *see*?'

'That it's an illogical warning when their own lord *is* the ruler of Melucha?'

'That, yes. But also, Amar's parents wouldn't think it was necessary to warn him not to meddle in affairs of state if they didn't believe he was doing it.'

'Try telling Kalban that,' Meenakshi said. 'Every time I read a book he warns me of the dangers of experimental Alchemy.'

'You're proving my point.'

'How does this help? Maybe he's scheming. Maybe not. But if he comes from a royal estate, that's the end of the theory that his landlord was using him as a spy.'

'I'm not so sure about that. Abhinav might use him to spy on Kalban, or the other way around. We'll discuss it later. Go on. Are there any more letters?'

'No.' Meenakshi shuffled through the remaining papers. 'Just more poetry.' She turned away from the desk.

Chitralekha was holding a long charcoal-coloured cloak.

'The person who came to tell me about Abhinav's hemlock purchase was wearing a cloak like that.'

'Was he?' Chitralekha shook out the cloak and held it away from her so she could look at it properly.

'That doesn't prove anything. Anyone might have a dark grey cloak. Kalban has a few, or at least he did in Madh. He used them when he wanted to disguise himself and eavesdrop on people on the streets.'

'It's unlikely that Kalban came hidden in a cloak to tell you something he could have told you in a normal way at a normal time, with a far greater likelihood of your believing him. And we're not interested in *anyone* who might own a cloak. We're interested in the people who were at dinner that night.' Chitralekha put the cloak back in the cupboard. 'I think we're done here.'

'Oh, I think you're not.'

Startled, they both turned to see Amar standing the doorway.

'I would ask why you're in my room, going through my possessions,' he said. 'But the answer is obvious. For some reason you've decided that you want to pin Kras's murder on me.'

'We don't want to pin it on anyone. We want the truth.'

'If you wanted the truth, and if you had a grain of sense, you'd be searching Varo's room, not mine.'

'Do you think Varo killed Kras?'

'I'm certain of it. Varo and Kras are old enemies. They've hated each other since long before you were born.'

'Why?'

'Who do you think it was who uncovered the plot to depose Shel? It was Varo. Why else do you think he found such favour at court? He didn't rise from commoner to Privy Councillor by ensuring that the roads and bridges were repaired.'

'*Varo* was the one who uncovered the plot—and told the Prince—but he didn't know Kras was involved, did he? Maybe he suspected, but he didn't have proof. He wouldn't have suppressed it if he had. That's why Kras kept his position.'

'Varo did have proof,' said Amar. 'He's been blackmailing Kras with it for years.'

'That sounds more like a motive for Kras to kill Varo than for Varo to kill Kras,' Meenakshi said.

'The proper procedure when Varo found out about Kras's involvement was to tell the Prince everything. He kept it back for the sake of filthy lucre.' Amar's fingers twitched. 'Where's a flute when you need one? The great Varo likes money just as much as any noble. He *needs* it more. Nobles have their estates to retire to when they get tired of court life. Varo has nothing. He had his eye on the position of Royal Tutor—I expect that's why he agreed to teach *you*. In ten or fifteen years he'd have had his fill of politics and been happy to settle into a sinecure. But if Kras had told anyone Varo was blackmailing him—and he might have done, now, with nothing to lose—that would have been the end of Varo's hopes.'

'Was he being honest?' Meenakshi asked, as they made their way—without sneaking, this time—back to her room. 'About Varo?'

'It's hard to say,' Chitralekha said. 'My senses are no good here. Everyone's lying and deceiving for *some* reason.'

'How do you suppose Amar knows, if it was such a secret? I can believe Rati knows.'

'I don't know that either. Maybe he overheard something. Maybe he was listening at doors. He seems to make a habit of it.'

'We're not in a position to judge,' Meenakshi pointed out. 'How much do you think he heard?'

Chitralekha thought for a moment. 'Not much,' she said at last. 'When you found the letter, I turned and I could see the door. He wasn't there. I turned back after you'd finished. He couldn't have been there longer than a few seconds.'

'I suppose that's something. Kalban's still going to lecture me.'

'Isn't it almost lunchtime?' Chitralekha asked. 'Go on, I'll wait in your room. I don't want to alarm the populace by going walkabout on my own. Bring Kalban after lunch and we'll ask him if he has any ideas about Amar.'

Kalban, when he came, was quite willing to believe that Amar was working in concert with *somebody*, but disclaimed any knowledge.

'I don't think it's important that my father owns the estate,' he said. 'Some of the smaller estates change hands every two or three years. You have the right idea with the letters. We need to speak to the person who delivers them. '

'How are letters delivered?'

'The couriers go around the estates and collect letters for Melucha, bring them here, wait in the city for a day or two and take the replies back. Important people have their letters delivered to their residence. Everyone else goes to the post inn. One courier might serve more than one estate—or a large estate might have several.'

'So Amar might be using several different couriers?'

'It's possible. We'll find out.'

'You make it sound so easy,' Meenakshi grumbled. 'Like we can send a crier through the streets asking for the courier who brings Amar's letters.'

'We can't do that, but we *can* ask the guards at the back gate.'

Kalban was firm in his insistence that Chitralekha would be causing undue agitation and also contravening several sections of the Inter-Realm Accord, by visiting the guardhouse, so she stayed in Meenakshi's room while he and Meenakshi went downstairs.

'We still don't know, do we?' Kalban asked. 'We've got someone else with good reason to kill Kras, and we're still no closer to knowing why it was done.'

'It seems to me,' said Meenakshi, 'that the man had a lot of enemies, and he was bound to be done away with sooner or later by one of them. That's the problem with Melucha. If you start education by teaching three-year-olds fifty different ways to eliminate their enemies, people will be eliminated.'

They'd reached the guardhouse, so Kalban didn't respond.

He rapped on the window. It was opened, and a grizzled head peered out. 'Pass?' it said. Then, 'Oh, excuse me, my lord. Are you expecting a visitor?'

'No, I wanted to talk to you about the couriers. Have they been coming in as usual?'

'Have your letters been delayed?' The guard withdrew his head. There was the sound of pages being turned. 'Very few couriers have been in this week. Ah, here's the list.' The head came back. 'There was a parcel for the Auditor of Expenditures—the courier came to deliver it to his office here because he couldn't find anybody at home.' The guard shook his head. 'Sad case, that. He's been going slowly mad for years. He thinks he's a merlin and keeps wandering around looking for his mews. It comes of reading foreign romances. Falconry has never been practiced in Melucha. The best he'll find is a disused stable.'

'What does the Auditor of Expenditures do?' Meenakshi whispered to Kalban.

'He's supposed to make certain officials don't misuse their allocated funds. He keeps tearing up the account books, so now the clerks make sure to keep a spare copy.'

'That was the only one,' the guard went on.

'Only one courier all week?' asked Kalban.

'I believe there's been some flooding on the road. The riders from the royal estates came through, but you must have received those letters. Were you expecting something else?'

'I'm not expecting anything. I want to know if there's been any unusual activity.'

'Oh.' The guard paused. '*That* sort of thing. The city couriers come through all the time. Perhaps you'll permit me to give you some advice, my lord.'

'What?' asked Kalban warily.

'You're not safe here. People are scared of magic. It's different for your mother. Now everyone's talking about a Celestial Dancer in the city. There's no shame in leaving, you know.'

'Do you think he's right?' Kalban demanded as they walked away. 'Should I just *leave*?'

'You want to stay, don't you, and lay your claims? I never thought you did in Madh, but now I do.'

'If nobody here likes me—'

'That's not important. There are plenty of people who don't like my father. Maybe you'll have problems—it seems like someone's trying to frame you for a murder—but so will you in Madh. If you *want* people to support your claim to the throne, fight for it.'

'How?'

'If I knew that, my uncle wouldn't have made me come here.'

CHAPTER XV

It had been a matter of debate who would go with Meenakshi to see Angana. Kalban was insistent that Chitralekha shouldn't go, because her presence could only bring about alarm and despondency. Chitralekha was equally insistent that she should, because she had centuries of experience dealing with mortals and their emotions, which was centuries more than Kalban, and in any case did Kalban think he could, by himself, ensure that Meenakshi didn't say anything unfortunate to the grieving widow?

Meenakshi had said that Angana might be a widow, but she hadn't seemed to be grief-stricken, which had resulted in both Kalban and Chitralekha telling her she knew nothing.

In the end, all three of them went to see Angana.

This part of the city was different from both the Old Town and the Tradesmen's Quarter. The houses, while not supplied with the high walls and guarded gates of the wealthy aristocrats, did have flower-bordered front lawns that were too large and green to be called yards. There was an occasional granite or sandstone sculpture to indicate houses that, while not yet supplied with marble nymphs, had intentions in that direction.

'Angana was given a house here after her family was stripped of their estates,' Kalban explained. 'It wouldn't have done to leave her with nothing. Penniless young women draw rebels like moths to a flame.'

'She wouldn't have been penniless. Kras had a decent income.'

'Nobody knew she'd marry him. Under normal circumstances her family would have seen to it that she was independent.'

'Did they have a house in the Old Town, too? What happened to it?'

'It would have become royal property. I expect my father gave it to someone he wanted to reward.'

'Varo?'

'He hasn't been *that* useful. Here we are.'

The carriage stopped outside a house that looked, in some indefinable way, more expensive than the others on the street. Two small nymphs, one carrying a book and the other an abacus, stood on either side of the path leading to the entrance. There was a wreath of deep red roses hanging from the front door.

'See? She's in mourning,' said Kalban, pointing to the wreath. 'Try not to upset her.'

'Allow me to remind you that she didn't want to see *you*.'

Angana came to the door herself. Unlike the previous day, she looked troubled, and as though she hadn't slept much.

'I thought you might come,' she said. Although she was addressing everyone, her gaze stayed fixed on Meenakshi.

‘I knew you would care about justice. I expect you have questions for me. Come in. I’ll help you in any way I can.’

They followed her into a sunny sitting room. Roses tucked into the pale grey ribbons holding back the curtains were the only signs of mourning. The upholstery was bright. The one painting in the room was a cheerful woodland scene.

‘I couldn’t afford to have everything redone,’ Angana explained. ‘Do sit down. I would offer you something to eat or drink, but if Kras had been alive . . .’ Her voice shook, ‘one of his first lessons to Meenakshi would have been on the inadvisability of accepting hospitality from strangers.’

Meenakshi felt uncomfortable—and it wasn’t the normal discomfort she felt in the presence of other people. Something was wrong.

Maybe it was the house. It was out of place. It was as though a house that should have been in the Old Town, with half a dozen Water-pot-bearing Maidens, had been divested of its glories and transplanted on to this quiet street.

Maybe it was Kras. Something of him seemed to linger. Meenakshi felt almost as though the padded armchair by the window was waiting for its master to return, to sit in it, perhaps to read a book or play the mandolin that now lay desolate beside it.

Kalban nudged her, and Meenakshi remembered herself enough to say, ‘I’m so sorry for your loss.’

That was probably something she should have said yesterday.

Angana nodded. ‘It was so wrong. All I want now is justice.’ I cannot allow Rati to—’ She stopped in confusion. ‘Forgive me. You asked me earlier whom I suspected, but I shouldn’t prejudice you. You must find the truth.’

'Can you tell us everything you remember about what happened the night he died?'

Meenakshi got another sharp nudge from Kalban. She ignored it. How would you get answers if you didn't ask questions?

Angana nodded again. 'I thought you might ask me that, so I've been trying to put it in order in my mind. We were the first to arrive—Kras wanted to speak to Kalban about your books, and he wanted to settle into his room. It had been arranged that he'd stay in his old quarters at the palace while he was teaching you.'

'You weren't going to stay?'

'It's been several years since I lived in the palace. I've found that I like having my own home, even if it lacks the royal comforts. And it was only going to be for a few months. We'd brought along some things Kras needed, his books and clothes, of course, his medicines—he tends to catch a chill in a north wind—and—'

Angana stopped, looking stricken.

'Yes?' Chitralekha prompted gently.

'And . . . no, nothing important. . . a painting I'd given him when we were married. He could never bear to part with it. I . . .'

Angana covered her face with her handkerchief. Meenakshi had never in her life felt so uncomfortable. She glanced around—she could climb out the window. It was a short drop to the ground. Kalban and Chitralekha could continue this conversation.

'No,' Chitralekha hissed under her breath.

After a moment, Angana lowered her handkerchief. Her face was dry, but drawn, as though she was under some great strain. Maybe it *was* grief; Meenakshi couldn't tell.

'Forgive me,' she said. 'I was overcome. Where was I?'

'You came early so Kras could settle in.'

'Yes, of course. He would be staying in our old suite, and I spent some time helping him arrange it. Nobody had used it since his retirement. It had been aired, of course, in preparation for his return, but there was still a slight musty smell. I . . .' She blushed. 'I asked the Princess to lend me some incense. It helped get the smell out.'

'What then?'

'We went down a little while before dinner. We were speaking to Varo—well, Kras was speaking to Varo. He wasn't interested in talking to me.' Angana gave a slight shiver. 'I've never liked that man. But I suppose he does *some* things well. They were discussing the intended curriculum. Later on, Rati and Dev arrived, and the court bard came in with them.'

'Did you speak to any of them?'

'Not that I remember. We went in to dinner soon after that. Rati wouldn't pay me much attention. I didn't expect otherwise. Once my notice would have been an honour—she would have jumped to do my bidding—but that is in the past. Now I'm nothing more than the wife—widow—of the Royal Tutor.'

Kalban shifted in his seat.

'After dinner we repaired to the library,' Angana went on. 'It was stuffy, even with the windows open. Kras finished his tea and then—he said he was tired—'

'You said he took some medicine,' Meenakshi said. 'Could the poison have been in that?'

'He didn't take his medicine that night. Do you think that made a difference? It was meant to be taken if he felt unwell, and he'd been in good spirits that day.'

'Are you sure he didn't take it? If you went home—'

'Oh, yes. He never took his medicine if he could avoid it. Most of the time I had to force it on him. He wouldn't have taken it of his own volition.'

'I don't suppose it matters. You didn't see anyone go near his cup of tea?'

'No, I didn't notice. I'm sorry.'

'It doesn't matter,' said Chitralekha. 'Can we see Kras's things? Especially the things he took to the palace with him? They may give us a clue to what happened.'

'Of course. I . . . I haven't yet had the heart to unpack what the Princess sent back from the palace. I had the boxes put in Kras's study. His personal effects are there. Come. I'll show you.'

She led them down the corridor to a large, airy room. Meenakshi noticed a distinct difference from the rest of the house. There was less elegance in this room, and, although it looked cheerful, it was undeniable that the upholstery clashed with the curtains. It was crammed full of books, papers and knick-knacks.

'You'll forgive me if I don't wait with you,' Angana said. 'It would be too difficult. The boxes from the palace are in the corner.'

'Of course,' Chitralekha told her. 'We understand.'

Meenakshi disagreed. She didn't understand at all. It made no sense to her that Angana could talk with reasonable composure about Kras's advanced age one day, and be unable to look at his writing paper without bursting into tears the next.

'We need to be methodical about it,' Kalban said, although he quailed as he looked at a tottering stack of books that came up to his shoulder. 'Meenakshi, you start with the bookshelf. You don't have to read the books. Just see if he's made any annotations or left any papers inside.'

‘I’m taking the palace crates,’ Chitralekha said.

‘I’ll deal with his desk.’

Chitralekha went to the crates. There was an inventory list attached to each. She opened the first one.

‘It’s already been opened,’ she announced. ‘I suppose Angana started and couldn’t bear to go on. It doesn’t seem like anything’s been taken out. It’s stacked to the very top.’

‘With what?’

‘These.’ Chitralekha held up a wooden box with an enamel design on the lid. A tiny latch held it shut. ‘Containers of herbs, according to the list. This one’s just got a bit of—some sort of dried plant thing? I want to say it’s ginger but the taxonomy of mortal flora isn’t my specialty.’

Meenakshi leaned over to look. ‘It’s dried ginger,’ she said. ‘I expect he had it for medicinal reasons.’

‘It’s odd that he’d take such a very tiny amount if he was planning to stay there a few months. But Angana did say he was neglectful about his medicine.’ She opened the next one, which was larger and round, with a top that screwed shut. ‘Oh, this one has ginger too. He must have kept most of it in this to keep its potency and a little in the other box to use.’

‘Keep going,’ said Kalban from the desk.

Meenakshi turned to the nearest bookshelf.

For several minutes they searched in silence. Then Kalban said, ‘I have something.’

Glad for the excuse to put down *The Ten Most Common Negotiation Tactics*, Meenakshi said, ‘What is it?’

‘A letter from Varo. Proof that Amar was telling the truth.’

'A *blackmail* letter?'

'Yes. There's a lot before and after. I'll read out the relevant part. *Let me now refer to the arrangement that we have had in place, to our mutual benefit, for several years. I fear the likelihood of the wrong person's learning of the indiscretions of your past is increasing. I can, of course, arrange for your safety, under the usual conditions. I understand that you may need some time to make the arrangements. We can speak about it at leisure.*'

'It doesn't fit with what Amar said. It gives Kras a motive to kill Varo, but not the other way around. And if Varo was afraid Kras would reveal information about him, why threaten him and make him angry?'

'Maybe he was trying to remind Kras that revelations could go both ways,' Kalban said, though he sounded doubtful.

'I have another letter,' Chitralekha announced. 'All the way at the bottom of this box. I *know* this one will interest you.'

'What does it say?'

'It's from our friend Rati, as I would have known even without her signature, because I can't imagine anyone else using this paper.' Chitralekha waved a translucent sheet with a pattern of swans around the edge. 'It goes on for six pages. I'll paraphrase. Kras got in touch with Rati because he was in urgent need of money—Varo's letter explains what the need was—and Rati is willing to give it to him, in exchange for his assistance in a matter that she will put before him at a suitable opportunity. That's clear enough.'

'Kras was going to start scheming again,' Kalban said. He sounded disappointed. 'He must have been desperate—but my father wouldn't care, now that it's been over for years. He isn't the type to bear a grudge.'

'No wonder he isn't a sorcerer,' Meenakshi said.

'Kras couldn't have been certain of your father's forgiveness in the matter,' said Chitralekha. 'Would you want to take the risk in his place?'

'I suppose not,' agreed Kalban. 'Does Rati give any indication of what assistance she wanted from Kras?'

'No, but she mentions the dinner—it must have been after you invited her. She doesn't seem to have expected Kras to be there.'

'I suppose she wanted to see what I was like first.'

'You thought you could bring her over to *your* side,' said Meenakshi. 'Didn't you? That's why you persuaded your father to invite her.'

'Yes, well, I was wrong,' Kalban snapped. 'There's no point discussing it. Let's get on with this.'

After another hour of searching, they had found nothing else of importance.

'I feel like we're missing something,' muttered Kalban.

'This isn't a room with secrets.' Meenakshi looked around. 'Your mother said the answer was in Kras himself, in his own character. I can't see it. His books are all . . .' She shrugged. '*Normal.* Nothing out of the ordinary, just endless volumes of political theory and philosophy . . .'

'Only those two subjects?' asked Chitralekha.

'There was also a biography of the late Maharaja—'

'You've been known to create alchemical beasts, Meenakshi,' said Chitralekha. 'How many bestiaries would one find in your bookshelf?'

'Alchemical bestiaries, you mean? I suppose it depends on which bookshelf. The one in my study has four, but I keep two in my bedroom, and there's another—'

'What Chitralekha is trying to say,' said Kalban, 'is that it's unlikely Kras was breeding scorpions.'

'Oh, yes, I suppose it is—' Meenakshi stopped short, her eyes widening. 'It *is* unlikely. It's *all* unlikely. Your mother was right! The answer was in Kras himself.'

'What?'

'Not just the scorpions. *Anyone* might breed scorpions. Why not? People in Vraja breed crocodiles. They're more dangerous. Scorpions don't drag you underwater and wait while you drown. Look *around*. The person who lived and worked in this room *couldn't* be the person who made the hidden room we found. He'd never be able to *focus* in a place like that. Kras's study is different from the rest of the house, so we can assume *this* is what Kras arranged the way he liked. If he'd had a secret lair, it wouldn't have had rows of jars smelling of bitumen and green goo oozing down the walls. It would have been secret, but bright and clean.'

'You're right,' Chitralekha said. 'But if it wasn't Kras—'

'There's one person that it's likely to have been. But I can't see what that has to do with everything else.'

Chapter XVI

'I don't think I'll ever understand people in Melucha.'

'I don't think,' Kalban told Meenakshi, 'you'll ever understand people anywhere.'

'Angana didn't ramble when I saw her in the palace. Or get upset.'

'Have you considered,' said Chitralekha, 'that she might feel more affected by her loss in the house where she lived with Kras than in the Lotus?'

'Could she really have had no idea of what Kras was doing? *Here* in Melucha? I can't even keep track of who was intriguing with whom!'

'Mortals,' said Chitralekha, 'like to delude themselves, especially about those they love.'

'It doesn't matter. I was silly to think Kalban's mother was talking about going through Kras's things, though that was useful so I'm not sorry we did. We've been—at least *I've* been—dealing with this like it was happening in Madh. If something's happened and you want to know who did it, first you trace the residues. And if you can't, you try to find the suspicious person—or the person with a motive.'

'That doesn't work here,' Kalban said. 'Everyone's suspicious. Everyone has a motive for offing everyone else.'

'Exactly. I should have realized that.'

'Do you have any idea now who might have done it?' Chitralekha asked.

'Not yet, but . . . *You* shouldn't have told lies. That makes everything harder.'

'I didn't lie.'

'Not outright. It would have *helped* if you'd told us everything. I wasted so much time trying to work out the logistics.'

Chitralekha smiled the rueful smile of the loser in a duel. 'Out of interest, when did you guess?'

'You said you had to report to Rambha.'

'Ah.'

'What are you two talking about?' asked Kalban.

Meenakshi started to reply, but Chitralekha said, 'Later,' indicating the front of the carriage, where the driver could hear every word through the thin wooden walls.

'How about the palace and the kitchen first?' asked Kalban. 'It's getting late. We can go to the shop tomorrow.'

Meenakshi thought for a moment and then nodded. 'In any case, if I find what I want in the kitchen, we may not need to go back to the shop. I'd rather avoid it. The clerk may not remember—I've been so *stupid*,' she murmured. 'Things are so different here.'

'Yes. They are.'

Meenakshi looked at Kalban sharply. Before she could say anything, Chitralekha said, 'You don't have to stay here if you hate it so much. I'm sure the Master Sorcerer will be happy to have you back for Fellowship studies.'

'You mean he'll be happy to have me back to deal with the paperwork from the Magical Activities Legislative Board. I'm not sure I want to *do* Fellowship studies,' said Kalban. 'Oh, I do like learning magic, but dedicating years of my life to experimental research? I wouldn't have time for . . .' he waved a hand around, 'this. It isn't—it never was—that I didn't like Melucha.'

'No,' said Meenakshi. 'You're afraid you won't find your place in it.'

'It's *difficult*.'

'How is it difficult? If anyone has a place, you do. You're the Prince-heir. Rati said the Privy Council is in favour of the rights of the firstborn. Unless you do something extraordinarily stupid, you'll be the next Prince.'

'Unless I do something extraordinarily stupid. Or unless Abhinav manages to drum up enough support among the nobles that the Privy Council is forced to change sides. Or unless one of Rati's schemes succeeds and I have to go into exile. Anything might happen.'

Gopali appeared from the antechamber off the main hall, where she had been waiting for them, and demanded Meenakshi's immediate presence in her room. Her glare took in Chitralekha and Kalban as well. They trooped after her.

'*This*,' hissed Gopali, as soon as they were inside, shutting and bolting the door. '*This* has gone far enough. I don't care who killed that doddering old fool. There must have been thousands of people who wanted to kill him. If I could go back in time, I'd do it a few days earlier so we wouldn't have to deal with this nonsense.'

'Has Varo been here again?' Meenakshi asked. 'Or the cloaked man?'

'Oh, no. Believe me, if Varo had been here and met me, he wouldn't have wanted to come back again in a hurry. Come here. Just *look* at what I found.'

She led them to the window, where, in a large glass tank, no fewer than a dozen scorpions were moving sluggishly about.

'Red scorpions,' said Kalban, equal parts horrified and fascinated. 'That's . . . how did . . . They're very rare! They've been impossible to get since Vraja clamped down on the export. *And* they're difficult to breed. There are very few people who could get hold of *one*. I don't know *anyone* who could get so many.'

'Do you have any idea how long it took me to catch them?' Gopali spat. 'I don't know if I got them all. I'm not sure there isn't one lurking somewhere in the curtains.'

'You managed to catch them without getting stung?' asked Kalban, deeply impressed. 'And you got them *alive*? It's one of the most deadly scorpion species known. Would you be interested in conducting a short course on catching scorpions, perhaps for members of the Privy Council?'

'I would be interested in leaving this place and going back to Madh.'

'But we're so close to knowing who murdered Kras,' Meenakshi protested.

'And do you want to be the next person murdered? It's clear that there's someone who doesn't want you to know who killed Kras. Even in this insane asylum disguised as a palace I'm sure people don't *want* their homicidal tendencies to become common knowledge.'

'Angana was right—he *does* deserve justice. Rati said he got what was coming to him for getting involved in politics again—but he had no choice. Varo was blackmailing him—'

'I *knew* Varo was odious,' Gopali snapped. 'Didn't I tell you he was odious? Murderers and blackmailers! What next? I was sent here for the express purpose of seeing that you stayed out of trouble. Someone released twelve fatal scorpions in your bedroom. That qualifies as trouble. Your uncle gave me the veto on this trip. I'm exercising it.'

'Yakshas and djinn are fatal too, but you never mind those.'

'Because you can handle yakshas and djinn. More to the point, one day it'll be your *job* to handle yakshas and djinn. You know nothing about scorpions—'

'I read the book!'

'*A Thousand Creatures Less than an Inch Long that Can Kill You*? It has half a page on red scorpions! And it *isn't* your job to deal with them, because, fortunately for us, you won't have to administer this madhouse.' Gopali transferred her baleful gaze to Chitralekha. '*You*. If you want to sort this out, do it yourself. Meenakshi isn't staying.'

‘It’ll be fine,’ said Kalban. He should have known better than to try to placate Gopali, who turned on him with such fury that he took a step back.

‘Fine? *Fine?* Are you not seeing the tank full of venomous insects?’

‘Not insects, arachnids—’

‘Yes, I called you in here to make sure I got the taxonomy right.’

‘There are still a few hours before Meenakshi has to go to bed,’ Kalban said. ‘I’ll tell the Palace Guard. They’ll have a Safety Officer sweep the room.’

‘And we’re staying,’ added Meenakshi. ‘Chitralekha promised to let me see her necklace if we solve Kras’s murder.’

‘*Did* she?’ Gopali said, as Chitralekha shrank back. ‘I have a thing or two to say to Chitralekha—’

‘I’ll be careful,’ Meenakshi promised.

Gopali scoffed. ‘How often have I heard something like that from you?’

‘Give us time,’ said Chitralekha. ‘I’m sorry about the scorpions. I didn’t think that would happen. I didn’t believe anyone in Melucha would care that much about being branded a murderer. But I need to find out who did it. For some reason people are willing to speak to Meenakshi, which is extraordinary, I agree, but there we are. And we *are* close.’

‘None of this is my problem.’

‘It *is* helpful to Meenakshi. She’s managed to speak to Kras’s widow—*twice*, so far—without offending her in any way. Would you have believed it possible?’ Gopali hesitated.

Chitralekha pressed her advantage. 'Asamanjas knows what Melucha is like. He still thought it was worthwhile sending her here. Another day, or two at the most, and we'll *know*. Then all you'll have to do is nag Meenakshi into writing essays for Varo and maybe dispose of an occasional viper. There'll be no swarms of scorpions.'

'Two days,' Gopali said. 'That's all I'm giving you. Forty-eight hours. If you haven't named a culprit in forty-eight hours, we're going home.'

'We'll take it.'

'And Kalban's going to get his Safety Officer to sweep the room morning and night. I'm taking no chances.'

As they made their way to the kitchen, it was Amar who stopped them. It was clear that he *hadn't* been lying in wait. He had the look of someone who'd been agonizing over whether to rhyme *dove* with *love*, or to go daringly for *move* instead, and had taken advantage of their passing to provide a welcome distraction.

'I know something you'll want to hear,' he said. 'That is, *if* you want to find out who killed the old man.'

'Proof against Varo?' Chitralekha asked.

'You could say that.' He opened the door to the room he'd been in, which appeared to have been set up for the express purpose of providing people with a location to plot. There was a single table with a dozen chairs around it. On the table were several sheets of paper with discarded attempts at a madrigal, but they could without difficulty have been replaced by blueprints showing secret alcoves from which poison darts could be shot. Although it was still daylight, heavy drapes over the windows blocked out most of the sun, allowing a single beam to run down the centre of the table.

Meenakshi was impressed. The Royal Academy operated on the dictum that atmosphere was everything. This room was teeming with atmosphere. If the Master of the Academy had been here, he would have hired the palace's interior decorator on the spot.

'Do take a seat,' Amar invited, sitting down himself. He pushed his chair back from the table. His face was in total darkness, which was pointless, since they knew who he was, but Meenakshi appreciated the effort.

When everyone was seated, Amar said, 'You didn't believe me when I told you Varo was a blackmailer. I knew you wouldn't. I investigated him myself.'

'You searched his room?'

'His office.' Amar held something up to the light. It was a velvet pouch of the variety that was meant to hold very expensive jewellery. 'I won't tell you what that is. See for yourself. I found this in his desk, pushed to the back. I suppose he didn't dare take it home. His wife's a decent woman. She wouldn't stand for such things.'

Chitralekha opened the pouch and shook it. Something bright and glittering fell into her hand.

'A brooch.' She held it so Meenakshi and Kalban could see. It was gold, with an intricate pattern of a ship worked in diamonds and sapphires.

'*Oh*,' Kalban said.

Amar nodded. 'You see? Now you know.'

'It's a coat of arms,' Kalban explained to Meenakshi and Chitralekha. 'It's not one I've seen before—'

'It's Angana's family's coat of arms. They made their money from their shipping interests. How would such a thing have come into Varo's possession? From Kras, who had to buy his silence and had nothing else left to give. Do you still think Varo wouldn't murder? He could take from Kras's wife the last keepsake of her family . . . I wouldn't put anything past him.'

Chitralekha put the brooch back in the pouch and tied it shut.

'You took it from his desk? He'll know it's gone.'

'He will, but what's he going to do about it? *Complain?* That'd mean admitting that he was blackmailing Kras—and keeping information from the Prince. He won't say a word. And it doesn't belong to him. Keep it. It might help with your investigation. You can return it to its rightful owner when you're done.'

Chapter XVII

'If anyone else interrupts us I'm going to open a portal back to Madh and step through,' Meenakshi said.

'Can we just get through the rest of the day without a disaster?' Kalban glanced out the window. 'They'll have started preparations for dinner.'

'Good,' Meenakshi said. 'We can go through unnoticed in the bustle.'

'You don't want to speak to Mada?'

'I've heard everything he wanted to tell me. I want to find out what he *didn't* say.'

Kalban led them through a tiny, unassuming door that opened into the passage leading from the kitchen to the storerooms. A couple of men were hurrying past carrying a large laden tray between them. A woman was scurrying in the other direction with a carafe. Nobody paid any attention to the new arrivals.

The storeroom was empty. There was a large sack next to the bin that had held Kras's tea.

Kalban knelt and sniffed at it. 'The new supply Mada ordered. We're just in time.'

Meenakshi opened the bin, scooped out a generous handful, and knotted it in her handkerchief.

'What's the point?' asked Kalban. 'We know whatever happened *must* have happened in the library.'

'Do we?'

'Mada ate and drank everything—'

'How do you know? Maybe he poured it into a convenient ewer. There's no shortage of them.'

Kalban stared at her. 'What aren't you telling me?'

'Not here,' Chitralekha began, but Meenakshi snapped her fingers, drawing a sound barrier around them. Then she explained as quickly as she could.

'Oh,' said Kalban, when Meenakshi had finished. '*Oh.*' He turned to Chitralekha. 'Is it *true*?'

Chitralekha had the grace to look abashed. 'I didn't *want* to keep it from you,' she said. 'I didn't know myself, at first—I don't keep track of *every* single one—and when I did find out . . . you're a murder suspect. I'm sorry, but you are. You know what regulations are like.'

Kalban shook his head. 'Yes, never mind. What now?'

'Now we'll go back, because it's almost time for dinner. You don't want to be late.'

Meenakshi's mind was racing as they took their places at the table. Handicapped though she was in areas such as guessing what people wanted and making the appropriate remarks when she encountered a classmate who had failed their last Alchemy practical and was despondent about it, she could follow a thread of reason. People seldom made sense to her: they were irrational and silly, but sometimes, like a new system of magic, a path of cause and effect lit up.

She was close. But something was missing.

Meenakshi was so lost in thought that Varo addressed her three times, and Kalban had to kick her under the table, before she remembered to answer him. He wanted to know if she'd decided on an essay subject.

'Er,' said Meenakshi, reflecting that this looked very much like ending the same way as her Negotiation lessons in Madh.

'Perhaps we should speak in greater detail about it at tomorrow's lesson,' said Varo.

'Of course,' Meenakshi agreed, though she doubted she would be any further along then.

She would test the tea in her skirt after dinner. She didn't know if there was a way to test for hemlock—other than the smell, and the strong odour of Kras's tea would negate *that*. She could try a history trace. But she'd need Kalban. She didn't know what a hemlock plant looked like. Maybe she could find a book that showed it.

'. . . and it will require considerable application of the theories you will read,' she heard.

'Oh,' she replied, her dejection deepening. She should have stayed in bed. Of course, then she would probably have been stung by a funnel-web spider concealed under her mattress.

The soup plates were cleared away and the next course arrived. Meenakshi glanced down the table at Mada. She could test her theory right now; nobody would have to know—

She heard a throat cleared and met Persis's eyes across the table. They were amused, but there was also a warning in them.

Meenakshi sighed. Things were easier in Madh.

Rati pushed her chair back as soon as she heard the bell chime.

'If it's the update from the palace, bring it in,' she called.

Dev, who had been punctuating mouthfuls of rice pudding with unflattering observations on the current exhibition at the Grand Gallery, got to his feet.

'Stay,' Rati said. 'This is important.' Dev sat back down.

The letter was brought in. Rati tore it open, quickly reading the few lines it contained.

'They went to see Angana this morning. Kras's wife,' she added, for Dev's benefit, because he liked to feign ignorance of anybody other than the members of the Council of Art. 'And looked through his things. Amar managed the business with the brooch.' She put down the letter. 'I knew he'd be a good ally.'

'Is that why you sound so pleased?'

'It's interesting that they went to see Angana. I wonder whose idea it was. Not the girl's—what did you think of her?' she demanded, with an abrupt change of subject.

'She seemed harmless. Foolish.'

'*You're* foolish if you think that. Don't you remember what Persis was like, before she decided to join civilization? Still, she's not as dangerous as she could be. I was . . . impressed, I admit, with what I saw of her when she was here. She was almost like one of us.'

'Are you coming around to the view that magic isn't evil?'

Rati laughed. 'Magic *isn't* evil. People are. Don't worry, I have no intention of making war on Madh. I'm . . . I hesitate to say it, but I'm beginning to think that even Kalban might have his uses.' Dev's eyes glittered with amusement. She added hastily, 'Not on the throne. Abhinav is better suited.'

'You won't try to kill him?'

'I already told you I don't kill children.'

'What about Kras? I asked you before, and you wouldn't answer me. Did you kill him?'

'I was nowhere near him all evening.'

When they were released from the library after dinner, a glance had Kalban following Meenakshi up to her room.

'How are you going to do it?' he asked. 'And I'm vetoing anything that includes the phrase *two-point time modification*.'

'How do you *ever* get things done?'

'Perfectly well, just like everyone else who doesn't feel the urge to solve simple problems with experimental magic. What's your plan?'

Meenakshi considered. 'Identifier spell,' she said. 'History traces are unreliable even without you being difficult about time modifications. Whoever put the snake in the bin must have left *something* we'll know them by.'

Kalban pursed his lips. 'Nothing is that simple. But go ahead and try.'

Meenakshi laid her handkerchief on the table and untied it. An assortment of shredded leaves, stems and flowers sat in a dull greyish-green heap.

'Do it quickly,' Kalban urged. 'Before Gopali comes back.'

'You're scared of *Gopali* now?'

'Of Gopali, no. Of what your uncle will say if she insists on going back before you've written a passable essay? Yes. And you *are* going to write a passable essay,' Kalban emphasized. 'Even if I have to stand over you and make you write it.'

There would be no getting away from the essay.

She gestured towards the scattered leaves, focused, and–

They separated into individual piles, translucent smoky forms twisting above each. After a few moments, they settled into a neat row of herbs, a scrap of cloth embroidered with animals, and one snake.

Kalban drew in his breath.

'Well?' Meenakshi demanded. 'Do you know whose it is?'

Kalban pointed at the second plant from the left. 'That one.'

'A plant that only grows in one garden in Melucha?' Meenakshi asked.

'It's hemlock.'

'Hemlock? You got so excited over *hemlock?*'

'It proves the tea was poisoned in the bin. We can stop worrying about who was standing by the window and who was looking at paintings and who might have hovered over Kras's shoulder with a phial. The main supply was poisoned.'

'Which means our list of suspects is much longer. This was supposed to *narrow it down*, not open it to anyone who might wander into the palace. What about that cloth?'

Kalban glanced at it. Then he said, 'Can you get more detail?'

'Not without magic you'd call dangerous. Why?'

'It looks like it came from a child's clothes. A ten-year-old at most. An adult wouldn't wear that pattern. Maybe just some tasteful elephants or peacocks, but not a *zoo*.'

'Who has a young child?'

'Rati and Dev—their daughter is too old for that, but they had another baby a few months ago. Rati was telling my mother about it.'

'Rati seems to be hiding something . . . Is it true that nobody other than Kras drank any of the tea?'

'If you'd ever tried it, you wouldn't ask,' Kalban said fervently. 'He made me try it once, when I was too young to know better. It's the foulest thing I've ever tasted, and that's including the time you used magic to make the thing you claimed was pea soup.'

'You see the problem? Somebody might have poisoned the supply years ago, intending it for Kras *then*—but he left. And whoever did it may have forgotten about it. Kras left in disgrace. Nobody would have expected him to come back. He *did*, and there was the tea still waiting—'

'And Kras drank it and died several years too late,' Kalban finished.

'Does hemlock lose its potency?'

'A little, but it doesn't become *safe*.' Kalban paused. 'Is that our conclusion? This was a tragic accident?'

'That's what I don't understand,' said Meenakshi. 'It doesn't feel like an accident. It feels . . . *meant*.'

'It *was* meant. The tea was intended for Kras and whoever put hemlock in it did intend to kill him. It just didn't work out at the time and the would-be murderer forgot about it.'

'They couldn't seriously have wanted to kill him, or they'd have found a way to do it after he retired. They wouldn't have sat around for years, waiting, on the off chance that he'd come back and drink the tea. Maybe they just wanted him out of the palace—'

'And he was safe as long as he stayed out.'

'Then the person who poisoned the tea might not be here anymore. It could be a footman he annoyed. And this is guesswork. Maybe someone went and mixed hemlock in with the tea when they heard Kras would be coming back—'

'Maybe it was Abhinav,' Kalban muttered. 'So what if he didn't buy the hemlock at the shop in the Tradesmen's Quarter? That doesn't mean he didn't get it somewhere else.'

'No,' Meenakshi said. 'We're going back to logistics and trying to recreate a crime scene. How will it help us if we go from shop to shop and get a list of everyone who bought hemlock at any time in the last twenty years? I'm sure a lot of those big mansions in the Old Town have a little patch in the garden.'

'You're right,' Kalban agreed. 'That isn't the way to do it. What is?'

'What your mother said—and what Angana said. Angana was talking about justice—and that's important—but she wasn't interested in proving *you* innocent. She wanted justice for Kras.'

'What do we know about Kras? Other than that he was scheming with Rati to put Abhinav on the throne?'

'You're not getting over that, are you? But you're right. He wasn't as *guileless* as everyone thought he ought to be. He was involved in Angana's parents attempted coup. I doubt he's kept his hands clean since then, though we may never know the precise details.'

'It's disappointing,' said Kalban. 'More than when I thought he really was on Abhinav's side.'

'Why? I thought you'd be pleased he didn't *like* Abhinav better.'

'At least when I thought he was on Abhinav's side because he believed Abhinav would do better, I thought he had *principles* . . . But it was to get himself out of trouble—trouble that he wouldn't have been in if he hadn't started interfering in the first place.'

'Why is it so bad for Kras to have interfered?' Meenakshi swept the leaves into one pile again and closed her hands around it. 'Everyone I've met seems to be scheming and plotting with somebody for something.' She lifted her hands. A pile of ash remained where the tea had been. 'Why is it so much worse for Kras than for any of the others?'

'It's because he was the Royal Tutor. He was supposed to prepare the heir for his place—whoever the heir might be—and serve the city and the common good, no matter who was ruling. He was meant to be *above* petty politics.'

'And that one thing led to everything else. If that's what it comes back to, the question we should be asking is why he got involved in the first place.'

Kalban considered that for some time. Then he said, 'You're right, and my father is the only one who might know, and who might tell us the truth. We can ask him in the morning.'

'First thing. The clock's ticking. I can't talk Gopali into staying if we don't find out who did it.'

CHAPTER XVIII

'Kras?' The Prince of Melucha sounded amused, weary and disinterested all at once. 'You want to know about Kras?' He surveyed Kalban and Meenakshi in silence. 'You will have to forgive my astonishment,' he said, his tone not astonished in the least. 'It has been our practice to handle our internal affairs, as one says, *internally*. We are not accustomed to this degree of interest from other realms.'

Meenakshi glanced at Kalban, who remained resolutely mute.

'Sit down,' said the Prince. 'I can see this won't be short.'

They sat.

'I understand,' he said, addressing himself to Meenakshi, 'that the Celestial Dancer is here to make certain my wife and elder son aren't murderers, and you're helping because Varo has decided that it's one way to let you learn how things work in Melucha. Have you learnt anything?'

'I've learnt that everyone is hiding something—and everyone wants something,' Meenakshi said.

'Then you have, at least, acquired the ability to distil years of experience into pithy sayings. I will not speculate on whether that will satisfy your uncle. As for your question, I assume you're referring to the rumours that Kras was involved with his father-in-law's plot to take the throne from me.'

'You *know* about that?'

'Everyone in the palace heard about it. There was no proof against him, and we like proof before we exile people.'

'Why did you let Kras stay on as tutor?'

'I wanted him where I could keep an eye on him. Would it have been wise to banish him and Angana to the countryside, where he could drum up support on the estates formerly belonging to his wife's family, rally the crowds to her cause and march on the city at the head of an unruly horde?'

'Was that likely?' asked Kalban.

'Who can say? It was a chaotic time. I was concerned about limiting the damage as much as possible. We took Angana's evidence first and sent her into the country, to one of the royal estates—not as a punishment,' he added. 'We believed she hadn't been involved, and thought it would be best for her to be away from the unpleasantness.'

'And by the time she came back it was all over?' asked Meenakshi.

'Yes. Her parents and brother had left. I believe they went to Vraja. I cannot be certain.' *That* must be a lie; Meenakshi could no more imagine Shel not being certain where his enemies were than she could imagine her father giving up his grudge against the Master of the Academy. 'We had stripped her father of his estates, so there was nothing for her to inherit—'

'Was that normal?'

'Oh, yes. If you're convicted of treason or sedition, everything is taken from you. It was hard luck on Angana. We arranged that she should have the property where she lives now. I believe it suits her. She also has a moderate income of her own from the Privy Purse. But none of this is helpful to you.'

'No. Why would Kras have become involved?'

'I thought at the time that he was content to be the Royal Tutor . . . He was starting to get on in years, but they sat lightly on him. His memory was sharp, and he was interested in his work—in learning, and in teaching. I did believe he was satisfied.'

'But he wasn't?'

'As time went by, he began to feel frustrated. Perhaps he felt he was starting at the beginning again with each generation. He had taught me, and I had become Prince, but he wouldn't be advising me as Prince—he'd be waiting for children to come so he could teach them the same things. It didn't occur to me. It should have done. That was a mistake.'

'Is that enough reason to plan a rebellion?' Kalban asked.

Shel sighed. 'I suppose it was too much to expect you to have done some research into the people you were attempting to reintroduce to the palace. Kras's family was once wealthy. Not aristocratic—there was no mansion in the Old Town, though his grandparents were great acquirers of studies in marble. His grandfather sat on the Privy Council as a representative of the city's merchants. They lent money to the city at need—at a profitable rate of interest.'

'What happened?'

'They lost their money. It happened many years before I was born. It was the result of a series of bad decisions. Kras's grandfather died young, and his grandmother had never been interested in the business. It fell to Kras's father, who did his best, but . . .' The Prince made a dismissive gesture. 'I always thought they took it very well. They managed to give Kras an excellent education—he studied Philosophy at the Academy in Madh. They had enough influence left to have him installed as the Royal Tutor.'

'Did Kras remember what it was like before his father lost his money?'

'He hadn't been born when it happened. He must have heard stories . . . and perhaps the solitary nature of his work led to his dwelling too much in the past. Maybe he thought he'd reclaim his family's old glories. It's sad, isn't it? I did feel sorry for him, which was why I let him stay.'

'Then he married Angana, and—were they happy?'

'Meenakshi,' hissed Kalban.

'It'll be helpful to know!'

The Prince gave Meenakshi a small smile. 'As far as I know, they were. I'm sure Angana missed her family, but she's pragmatic. She found other interests to fill her days.'

'Who do you think killed Kras?' Meenakshi asked.

'If I had to lay a wager, it would be on Abhinav. Abhinav hated Kras.'

Kalban looked startled. 'I thought—'

'You thought they got on well? They did, on the surface. But Abhinav sensed something of Kras's bitterness and resentment, and he didn't know enough of his history to feel sorry for him.'

'Was that why Kras had to go? It wasn't just about giving information to Rati?'

'That would have been enough on its own, but I wasn't sorry to have an excuse to dismiss him. There would have been a tragedy of some sort if he'd stayed. Abhinav's dislike was becoming more and more apparent, and Kras was becoming ill tempered in his old age. And he *was* old enough to be pensioned off. If he'd gone quietly it would have saved a lot of trouble, but he dug his heels in and insisted Royal Tutor was a position for life. I needed to come up with something.'

'Did Abhinav hate Kras enough to kill him when he came back—even if it was only going to be for a few months?'

'Abhinav knew Kras would be angling to be appointed Royal Tutor again, and couldn't bear the thought of having him hanging about the place. He wouldn't have had any lessons with him, but Abhinav couldn't stand the sight of his face.'

Kalban glanced at Meenakshi. 'If you're thinking what I think you are . . .'

'I am.'

'Abhinav might have forgotten.'

Meenakshi laughed. 'Not him! And you're supposed to be the one who knows people. He'd never forget a thing like that.' She glanced at the Prince. 'Would he?'

'I have no idea what you're talking about, but I suspect, if I did, I would agree with you.'

'Are we missing something?' Chitralekha asked. 'I feel like we are.'

'Maybe we'll get a confession from the murderer,' Kalban said, though he didn't sound very hopeful.

'We haven't cleared out the secret room yet,' Meenakshi said suddenly. 'Let's go search. We may find the proof we need. I didn't look at anything closely last time—I didn't want to.'

'How will that help? The law against scorpion breeding hasn't been passed. It's bad form to do it in a secret room off somebody else's bedroom, but nobody's going to charge anyone with a crime over it.'

Meenakshi was staring at him with the astonished expression that was infuriatingly familiar. It meant she couldn't believe he hadn't made some connection that ought to be self-evident to anyone who wasn't an imbecile, but she wasn't saying it because she'd been told enough times that it wasn't polite.

'What?' Kalban asked.

'You said yourself that red scorpions are rare and Vraja has clamped down on exports. Who's likelier to have that many to spare than someone who breeds scorpions?'

'Maybe,' Kalban said. 'But the room was abandoned years ago.'

'The breeding may have moved somewhere else. We can search, anyway. How would it hurt?'

'We can search,' Kalban agreed. 'I want to clear out the room.'

Meenakshi looked around the room with a silent shudder. She had remembered it as being dank and depressing, with unpleasant things oozing down the walls. Her memory hadn't deceived her. She conjured a few glowing orbs to sit in the sconces. They did little to brighten the gloom.

'Do you want to burn this?' Chitralekha asked.

'I thought we could, but it'll take forever. And we'll have to deal with the jars.'

'Isn't there a museum you could donate the things to? Or maybe the Zoology lab at the Academy?'

Kalban shook his head. 'I would only donate this to someone if I hated them and wanted to give them nightmares. I agree we can't throw them wholesale into the fire—'

'With all that embalming fluid?' Meenakshi scoffed. 'Even with a contained magic fire, we'd risk burning the place down. We'll have to do it slowly.'

'Do you have any ideas? One thing I can tell you, it's not staying here.'

'Have it sent to the Privy Council,' Meenakshi suggested. 'They're debating scorpion breeding regulations. They might as well see some examples.'

'There are other things too,' said Kalban, shivering as his eye fell on a viper with fangs the size of daggers. 'You're right. I'll send it all to the Privy Council, except the books. Those I'll send your father. At least then the Privy Council will know I'm serious,' he added in a mutter.

'Serious about what?' asked Chitralekha.

'Serious, in general. Not someone to be trifled with or taken lightly.'

'Let's start with the books,' said Chitralekha. 'We can stack them in a corner of Kalban's room and take them to Gopali later. She can pack them up to send to Madh.'

'Great, let's give Gopali another reason to hurry Meenakshi back,' Kalban muttered. 'Asamanjas will be thrilled with me.'

'She won't mind the books.' Meenakshi, having taken *Spellwork to Conceal Your Guilt* from a shelf, was already snickering as she flicked through it. 'You should see the illustration of an Illusion in this. You'd give yourself apoplexy if you followed these instructions.'

'That doesn't tell us anything useful.'

'It tells us that whoever collected these books knew nothing about magic,' Meenakshi countered. 'So it's unlikely to have been your mother. These people have been under the impression that magic is anything from an outdated tome with lots of pentagrams on the inside cover and . . .' She laughed outright as she glanced at the last page. 'A list of disclaimers about the terrible things that happen to you if you do it wrong. That's accurate, at least.'

'Just about anyone in Melucha might fit that description.'

Meenakshi released the book, which floated out into Kalban's bedroom and settled itself on the floor in a corner by the window.

'Where do you suppose these came from?' Chitralekha asked. She was leafing through a book whose title Kalban couldn't see, but whose leather binding was covered in dark splotches. 'Has someone been raiding used bookshops?'

'Disreputable used bookshops, maybe,' said Meenakshi, sending three more volumes to join *Spellwork to Conceal Your Guilt*. 'Should we send the jars through the Privy Council meeting room windows?'

Kalban stifled a laugh. 'As appealing as I find the prospect of sending the Privy Council into fits, no. They won't vote for me if I shock years off their lives. I'll start stacking them up on the opposite wall—there are fewer of them than the books—and I'll have someone take them down tomorrow.'

'You just don't want to look at the books,' Chitralekha said.

'You're right, I don't. They're creepy. The sooner they're out of here, the better.'

'If you feel that strongly about it, why wait for Gopali to pack them? I can open a portal and send them through once we're done.'

'We'll have to fill a form,' Kalban began.

'Then we'll leave them here,' said Meenakshi. 'I'll let Gopali know and she'll come by for them when she's free. If she's still angry about the scorpions, that might not be for another week.'

'Fine, open the portal. The Portals Regulation Desk never has anyone on it anyway. They won't notice.'

'It's odd,' said Meenakshi. 'The number of laws you have against magic in Melucha with nobody to enforce them. Most of the time you rely on people's goodwill.'

'Goodwill, not wanting to be pitchforked by an angry mob. Pick one.'

For some time they worked in silence. Then Chitralekha said, 'If most people think magic is terrible, why would these books be available here?'

'They're old books,' said Kalban. 'And magic is *regulated*, not banned. People don't think it's *evil*. They're just . . . uncomfortable with it.'

'Like thunderstorms,' agreed Meenakshi. When Chitralekha stared at her, she added, 'You never know what a thunderstorm will do—and there's so much energy in the air—but there's something . . . friendly . . . about them.'

'Friendly?'

'They're like people. Sometimes more than people are.'

Chitralekha transferred her astonished stare to Kalban, who said, 'Ignore her. Meenakshi doesn't know anything about how people are.'

'I'm just saying—oh, this is odd.'

'What?'

'It's a record of magical activity . . .' Meenakshi flicked pages. 'It goes back about two hundred years. Not real magical activity, most of it. It's silly things like someone's cat looked at someone else and then the other person tripped over a tree root and twisted their ankle.'

'Oh. All estates used to keep those records once. It was mandated by law. It stopped in my great-grandmother's time. These books must be from someone's private collection.'

'Whose?'

'All the noble families have libraries, and a lot of them have rubbish like this, because they've been collecting for decades, if not centuries. These days people have been selling off the obsolete books to raise money. They're popular with collectors. You need additional income to run the estates now that you can't tax tenants so heavily—'

'One of the estates?' said Meenakshi.

'Yes, why?'

'This book has a map. Do you want to see?'

Kalban nearly dropped the jar he was holding in his haste.

Chapter XIX

'So we'll meet Gopali's deadline.'

'Remember, I get that necklace for a week,' said Meenakshi, as she put the last of the books on the pile. 'Where should we leave them? I can send them straight into Father's study and leave a note.'

'Put them in your study,' Kalban said. 'And write to Saha. She'll see them delivered—and she'll keep my name out of it.' The record book was in his hands. 'Are we sure this is going to work? It's just . . . just so vague. We could be wrong.'

'We could be,' agreed Meenakshi. 'Do you think we are?'

'No, I think we're right. It fits. But we have no proof.'

'True enough,' Chitralekha said. 'And *I* need proof, if Melucha doesn't.'

'I don't think that'll be a *problem*. If we're right, we'll have the proof we need at tomorrow's Privy Council meeting.'

‘Rati will be there anyway,’ said Kalban. ‘Should we ask father if he’ll invite Angana? She did want justice. I’m sure she’ll want to see it done.’

‘Why not?’ Meenakshi murmured. ‘And we can get the head of the kitchen to come up too. He has something to answer for.’

‘You’re overreacting,’ said Chitralekha.

‘At the very least, Mada has lied. Besides, he won’t be able to stay on once the truth is known. There’s no point in delaying these things. Best to do it all in one go.’

‘Nobody can say you hesitate to cause trouble,’ Kalban said. ‘You speak to Mada, I’ll speak to my father and Chitralekha can wait. Unless you want to take the chance to see the city? After tomorrow you won’t have legitimate business here. If you want to take in the Grand Gallery, today’s the day.’

‘Why are you suddenly not worried about my going out in public?’

‘It doesn’t matter, if things go as planned tomorrow.’

‘Well done,’ said Chitralekha. ‘You’ve taken your first step to getting some popular support.’

‘I’m not so sure I want that. But,’ Kalban went on, with uncharacteristic laxness, ‘there’ll be time to worry about that later. After,’ he continued, with a return to his usual manner, ‘we’ve persuaded Gopali that the danger is past and it’s safe to stay. I don’t want Asamanjas writing me reams about how disappointed he is.’

They parted after lunch. Kalban went to speak to his father, and Chitralekha left to examine the works of art in the gallery. Meenakshi made her way back to the kitchen, this time entering through the large door leading into the garden. It was quiet.

Meenakshi found Mada in the back of the kitchen, poring over a sheet of paper while a terrified underling trembled at every frown that crossed his face.

'You again?' he said when he saw her. 'You'll have to wait. I need to make some adjustments to the dinner menu. This one is unimaginative.' There was a squeak from the man next to him. 'Radishes make no sense. Even *you* must see that.'

Meenakshi, who had never given much thought to how much sense radishes made, could only murmur something non-committal. Fortunately, he wasn't interested in her response. After several moments that were clearly agonizing for his assistant, he made some notes on the paper.

'Here,' he said. 'Start preparations as usual. I hope I won't have to ask for anything to be redone. And someone needs to visit the market this evening.' At last, he returned his attention to Meenakshi. 'Well? What do you want?'

'I believe I know what happened the night Kras died,' said Meenakshi. 'And, more importantly, how it happened.'

'Is the *how* more important?'

'It was to me. *What* happened wasn't hard—someone poisoned him. But I was spending my time worrying about people walking around the library and whether Kras would have watched his cup every moment—whether the people would have watched each other—whether *you* would have watched Kras's cup. That was always the problem. It wasn't whether Kras was poisoned, because we know he was, but *how* he was poisoned.'

'And now you know?' asked the head of the kitchen, looking at Meenakshi much as he had looked at the paper about radishes.

'I think I do.'

'Come inside. We should speak in privacy.'

He led Meenakshi into what was evidently his personal room. It had a low table covered in an array of knives. Bunches of herbs hung from the ceiling.

'You know who did it,' he said. 'Then why are you here wasting my time?'

'I want to know why you encouraged us to look at your old tea samples and wonder about who had been in the storage area, when you knew that didn't matter.'

'Didn't it?'

'You don't scare me,' said Meenakshi. 'I know the rules. There was hemlock in the tea. Already in the tea. And *you* knew. With everything that's at stake, I doubt anything happens here without your realizing it. You *chose* not to tell anyone.'

'I have some sympathies in this matter.'

'*Why?*'

'I don't have to explain myself to anyone—to you least of all.'

'Consider it practice. You're going to have to do a *lot* of explaining soon.'

'You wouldn't understand if I *did* explain. Do you know what it was like, sitting through meal after meal with nobody paying me any more attention than if I'd been a part of the furniture, when all the time –'

He broke off.

‘All the time?’ Meenakshi prompted.

‘It isn’t easy to stay out of things.’

‘That seems to be the common thread running through this,’ said Meenakshi.

‘Whatever you may have heard, Kras wasn’t a good person. I’m not blaming him. He never had a chance.’

‘How would *you* know what sort of person he was? You’ve only been here a few months, and you saw him once.’

‘I didn’t need to see him. When someone’s lived somewhere as long as Kras had in the palace, they leave traces of themselves behind. They’re in the people who knew them and dealt with them every day—and how they’re remembered by those people. Kras grew bitter and resentful as the years passed and he realized he couldn’t recover his family’s old position just by being the Royal Tutor.’

‘You said it yourself. He never had a chance.’

‘I was trying to be generous. He might have had a chance if he’d allowed himself one. He was obsessed with returning to the past. If he’d given more thought to his future he might have succeeded in gaining something.’

‘Does that make you feel better about not *trying* to save his life?’

‘I did my duty,’ said Mada. ‘I watched. I am not the head of the safety team or the captain of the palace guard. Once Kras made the decision to return to the palace, he was never going to live long. And his safety . . . well, *that’s* not my primary responsibility.’

‘Even *I* know that’s antisocial,’ Meenakshi said. ‘You could have prevented Kras’s death.’

'That day, by *that* hemlock, yes, I could have done. Kras, as I'm sure you've realized by now, was a man who made enemies. If he'd stayed in his retired life, content to live out his days in peace, he might have been safe. Once he returned to the palace . . . at least, this way, he died in his bed.'

Chapter XX

'Are you sure?' Kalban asked, because he knew the question would annoy Meenakshi.

She glared at him. 'If you want me to be *sure*, you'll have to let me Scry into the past so we can *see* what happened. But it's *very* likely that our theory is correct.'

'We'll just have to do our best.' Kalban wrapped the last of the jars in cotton wool and lowered it into the crate he had brought to his room. He added, after he straightened, 'that might work well.'

After all, the disinterested air of stating facts and having little to no concern about how they affected people, which was Meenakshi's normal method of addressing strangers, tended to be very effective at persuading the strangers she addressed that lies were futile.

Meenakshi waved and the lid settled over the crate. 'Do we need to nail it shut?' she asked.

'No, just hold it with magic. We want to be able to open it in a hurry and we *don't* want to waste the Privy Council's time prying out nails.'

'All set?'

'Yes. Let's go.'

Two members of the palace guard were waiting outside. Kalban called them in. They loaded the crate on to a trolley and wheeled it away.

'They'll meet us in the chamber,' Kalban said. 'Are you *certain*?'

'Are you going to keep asking that until I lose my temper?'

Kalban sighed. 'Let's go.'

There was some trouble at the door to the council chamber, where the guards insisted that only Kalban could go inside, and that Meenakshi should go to the visitors' gallery and Chitralekha somewhere else, preferably back to the Inter-Realm. No amount of argument from Kalban made a difference.

Meenakshi was on the verge of opening a portal into the chamber when the door opened and the Prince looked out.

'Let them in,' he ordered.

Meenakshi was amazed at the expedition with which he was obeyed.

Most of the Privy Council had already assembled and were going through their order papers. They looked up with expressions ranging from disapproval to hostility.

'I must apologize,' said the Prince. He turned to Kalban. 'I'm sure you have an excellent reason for these flagrant breaches of protocol. I do hope you plan to share it with us.'

'Yes,' said Kalban. 'We do have a reason.' He glanced towards the viewing gallery, where Angana stood. 'Perhaps you'd like to join us?'

Angana came down the stairs, followed, uninvited, by Dev.

Shel turned to one of his attendants. 'Go and see if there's anyone else in the gallery. If so, they can wait outside.' As the attendant hurried up the stairs to do his bidding, Shel turned to Kalban with a sigh. 'We're going to have to stop having people over for dinner. It's not worth the subsequent commotion. Get on with it. I suppose you know who is responsible for Kras's death?'

'That depends,' said Meenakshi, 'on how you define responsibility. I'll tell you what we *do* know, and you can decide.'

'I look forward to it. We had so little on our schedule this morning, I was wondering how we'd fill the time.'

'The mistake I made when we started,' said Meenakshi, on whom sarcasm was wasted, 'was worrying about the *logistics* of how Kras died. *Then* I tried to think about who might have had a motive to kill him—which was stupid. Everyone had a motive to kill Kras.'

'Oh?'

'Varo was the first to bring up motives. He told me Rati and Dev were plotting to put Abhinav on the throne, and Kras, who had originally been involved, had decided he couldn't help them anymore. That seemed like a slim reason to kill him, but maybe they thought he'd ruin their plans by revealing them to Kalban? That, at least, was possible.'

Rati smiled at Meenakshi. 'I knew we'd get along if you overcame your prejudices. I like a smart girl.'

'Abhinav,' Meenakshi went on, ignoring her, 'as we were told by Abhinav's father, hated Kras. He might have been willing to leave him in peace, as long as he stayed in retirement and Abhinav could forget his existence, but he couldn't have him in the palace again. In most places, disliking someone isn't enough reason to kill them. But if you teach the alphabet out of a book that informs impressionable children that H is for Hemlock, you shouldn't be surprised if, as Kras did, you find it in your tea. I *did* think that Abhinav must have known Kras was plotting in his favour—and I thought that would have influenced him to *like* Kras. Maybe I was wrong,' Meenakshi added, glancing at Abhinav.

'I'm all for people plotting on my behalf,' said Abhinav. 'Kras *wasn't* plotting on my behalf. I found out what he was doing before my father sent him away. He thought he'd be able to control me if I owed my position to him. He couldn't take the throne himself, so he wanted to be the power behind it. I couldn't have stood for that.'

'All right,' said Meenakshi, who hadn't listened to a word. 'That puzzled me, but if that's the way you feel about it . . . There you go. Abhinav had a motive, because . . . Kras wanted to help him rule?' Meenakshi glanced at Kalban. 'Not important. When we were going through his room, we found a bill of purchase for hemlock, dated shortly before the dinner.'

'I'd like to point out that I wouldn't be stupid enough to buy hemlock in order to poison someone, poison them and leave the bill of purchase in my room to be found days later by someone investigating the death.'

'That's what Kalban said,' agreed Meenakshi. 'Someone *else*, under the impression that I had contracted a sudden case of amnesia, came to my room in the middle of the night to tell me he'd seen Abhinav buying hemlock at a shop in the Tradesmen's Quarter.'

'Who was it?' asked Rati.

'We'll come to that. Kalban and I visited the shop. Abhinav *had* purchased hemlock, but the clerk was very careful to tell us that it was a new hybrid that was far more fast-acting than normal hemlock. We knew that wasn't in Kras's cup, since he retired to his room without arousing anybody's suspicions—so we could only assume that Abhinav had purchased the hemlock intending to murder someone else, a murder that hasn't yet happened.'

'It was general supply,' said Abhinav.

'It's normal to have a general supply of hemlock, but for some reason the most basic spells are forbidden.' Kalban glared at her, and she went on hastily, 'That's beside the point. It brought up the idea that Abhinav had an enemy who wanted him blamed for the murder.'

'He had an enemy, then, who knew nothing of Melucha,' said Shel, 'if he thought Abhinav would be *blamed* for murder, particularly when the victim has . . .' He trailed off with a smile.

'*When the victim has been dabbling in politics himself*,' finished Meenakshi. 'Is that what you were going to say? It's bad form to murder a non-combatant, which Kras . . . well, we heard conflicting accounts. Many people seemed to think that, although nothing had been proven against him, Kras *had* done things that could be construed as entering politics of his own volition. So he had no grounds to complain if it ended in trouble.'

'Quite right,' came a mutter from one of the Privy Councillors whom Meenakshi didn't know. 'That's the sensible view.'

'Everyone pointed us in a different direction. At first I thought there was a concerted attempt to protect the killer, but that wasn't true. Most people really didn't know who'd killed Kras and were guessing. But there *were* two individuals, other than the murderer, who knew—and who *did* conceal the truth, one actively, the other through omission.'

'Now it's getting interesting,' Abhinav said, grinning.

'The first of these people was Amar,' Meenakshi said. The court bard raised an eyebrow. 'He was the one who came to my room wrapped in his cloak to tell me Abhinav had been buying hemlock.'

'Perhaps my understanding is flawed,' said Shel. 'That sounds very little like *concealing* the truth. He told you what he saw—and you say it was true.'

'He told me *a* truth, thereby concealing *the* truth. Abhinav had bought hemlock. It was the wrong hemlock. Illogical as it was, that made us shift our attention from Abhinav. That's something Amar relied on. A good court bard knows how to make people ignore details he doesn't like. Kalban had been *convinced* that Abhinav was the murderer, and Chitralekha and I had both been a bit sceptical. The clerk's evidence seemed to clinch it. Abhinav couldn't have killed Kras with the hemlock he bought.'

'Who was the other person who concealed the truth?'

Meenakshi glanced at the head of the kitchen, who had been silent.

'*You?*' said Shel, sounding for the first time as though he hadn't already read the script. 'What did *you* lie about?'

'I didn't lie,' said Mada, far politer to the Prince than he had been to Meenakshi. 'But she's right. I didn't tell her everything.'

'What didn't you tell her?'

Mada hesitated.

'There's no point,' Meenakshi said. 'You can't do this job any longer. Your judgement has been compromised. You'll have to go.'

'If you won't see my side of it, I don't have a choice. I'll let you explain.'

'I spent so long,' Meenakshi said, 'trying to work out *who* could have put poison in Kras's cup in the library—because I knew Mada had had a cup of tea from the same pot, and shown no ill effects.'

'So he didn't drink the tea?' Abhinav asked. 'What did he do? Pour it into a convenient vase? Someone would have noticed.'

'Oh, no, he drank the tea. It was the bracelets that gave him away. Whenever I see him at the table, he's always fiddling with them. It's irritating. I frequently have the urge to rip them off him and turn them into lead.'

'I frequently have the same urge,' Abhinav said. 'Except turning them into lead, which I have no idea how to do. I want to throw them out the window.'

'When I went to see him in the kitchen, he didn't have any nervous habits. And then . . . well, I realized when Chitralekha showed me her necklace.' Meenakshi glanced from Chitralekha to Mada. 'It's the stones. As soon as I saw hers—he uses it to communicate with the Inter-Realm.' At the blank expression of some members of the Privy Council, Meenakshi explained, 'He's not mortal. He's a Sprite. He came here just before Kalban returned from Madh.'

'We're in murky waters now.' If Shel was surprised, he managed not to let it show beyond a strained smile. 'Is he—' He turned to Mada. 'Are you a Sprite?'

'I am,' said Mada. A change came over him. He looked less human, his features sharper, his skin alight with a golden glow.

'It's official. As long as Kalban was in Madh, Melucha wasn't considered a serious threat—the only practitioner of magic of some power here was Persis. We could keep an eye on her magical usage, which tended to stay steady, and low.'

'Kalban was in Madh,' added Chitralekha, 'which we monitor closely in any case. Once he moved to Melucha, we needed someone on the spot.'

'You helpfully got rid of the head of your kitchen—'

'She retired,' hissed a member of the Privy Council, awakening at last to the fact that there was a previously unidentified Immortal being in the room with him.

'Retired, then. She was gone, the position was open.'

'And,' added Meenakshi, 'Sprites, like most beings from the Inter-Realm, are immune to mortal poisons. Of course, he would take particular care that nothing untoward happened—but he did it by watching everyone, *all* the time. Having him taste things was pointless. He could have garnished all his soups with hemlock without suffering any ill effects.'

'I wouldn't do that. It tastes as foul as the old tutor's tea.'

'In the light of this disturbing information,' Shel said, 'I'm going to have to write a strongly worded letter to Urvashi. I cannot have unauthorized Immortal beings in my city.'

The now-former head of the kitchen shrugged. 'I doubt you'll get far. The Inter-Realm Accord allows it, as long as both Kalban and Persis live here. If it's any consolation, the next one won't be working in the kitchen.'

'You will find,' said Shel, his smile easing into something far more unsettling, 'that the Prince of a sovereign state can exclude anybody that he wishes, including and most especially unidentified Sprites. If the Inter-Realm Accord does not allow for this, we may need to reconsider some of its provisions.'

'Urvashi will be *furious* with Mada for getting caught,' Chitralekha whispered gleefully in Meenakshi's ear.

'Can we retroactively refuse to ratify the treaty?' asked one of the Councillors.

'No, no, we should go to the source and file a complaint.'

'The *source*? You want to visit the Inter-Realm?'

'Why not? They seem to come here as though we're a public watering hole!'

'Ladies, gentlemen, please,' Shel said. 'I'm as outraged as you are, but I assure you that the matter will be dealt with. Let's keep to the main issue.'

'Yes,' said Angana. There were two spots of colour in her cheeks. 'You promised me justice.'

CHAPTER XXI

‘I *don’t* think,’ Meenakshi said, ‘that Abhinav hated Kras so much that as soon as he heard he was coming to dinner, he went out, bought hemlock, and put it in the tea. Amar put that idea in my head—knowing it was wrong—precisely so I’d focus on other people once I realized it *was* wrong.’

‘You’ll have to explain more,’ said Shel.

‘Abhinav *did* put hemlock in Kras’s tea—years ago. I’ve told Kalban plenty of times that you should teach children that H is for Horse, or Hat, or something innocuous like that—oh, I don’t mean the book. This is how the court of Melucha works. Abhinav realized that Kras was plotting to put him on the throne for the *wrong* reasons, and instead of having him dismissed he decided to try to kill him.’

‘I don’t *try* to kill people,’ Abhinav said, producing his dagger from his sleeve and twirling it in a manner that seemed likely to cost him a thumb. ‘If I wanted someone dead, he wouldn’t be available to teach you Political Science years later.’

'Wouldn't that depend on how badly you wanted him dead? Kras left—your father dismissed him—before anything happened. Your father knew, not exactly what you'd done, but that you'd done *something*. He felt sorry for Kras, and wanted him out of the way. Once he was gone, you didn't care enough to go after him. The hemlock stayed mixed with the tea in the big bin downstairs, because nobody ever drank Kras's tea.'

'I admit everything.'

'You heard Kras was coming back. You *wouldn't* have gone to get new hemlock to kill him. He wasn't that important. Would you have done anything about the hemlock that was already there? I think not.'

'It was fate. When I first slipped into the kitchen and poured the hemlock in the bin of tea, it wasn't Kras's time. He left. When it *was* his time, he came back to his own doom. I didn't have to do anything.'

'Amar is your friend. You came up with the plan of going and buying new hemlock in case it became necessary, as it later did, to divert suspicion.'

'You have to admit it was a good plan.'

'I absolve Mada of blame in this—he *didn't* know that there'd been hemlock in that tea. If it did smell of hemlock, it was faint—I couldn't tell myself—and Mada had never seen or tried the tea before. He knew it only by reputation.'

'So . . . *Abhinav* killed my husband?' Angana had a very odd expression on her face, like someone waking from a nightmare. 'Abhinav did it?'

'Yes,' said Abhinav, sounding, for the first time, a little regretful. 'I did.'

'No,' Meenakshi said. 'You didn't.'

Abhinav's expression of irritated displeasure was identical to his father's; Meenakshi could understand why those who had prospered under Shel's rule wanted his younger son to take his place.

'Didn't you spend the last fifteen minutes lecturing everyone on how you found out I was guilty?'

'You are, if intent is guilt. You meant to kill him—or, at any rate, you knew it was likely he would die and you didn't try to prevent it. But intent to commit murder *isn't* the same as committing murder. The fact is that Kras didn't die because of your actions.'

'What happened to him?'

'Murder isn't the only crime people commit,' Meenakshi said. 'There's also blackmail.'

'Do explain.'

'Chitralekha ought to have been able to judge who had malicious intent, but she couldn't in Melucha because, according to her, everyone did. Was that why a Sprite was sent down instead of a Dancer? They rely less on their instinct for what people are feeling and more on. . .'

'The science of human nature,' said Mada. 'The Dancers' arts belong to the past. Psychology is the future.'

Chitralekha responded with an icy glare that would have done Urvashi proud.

'Chitralekha couldn't help us,' Meenakshi went on. 'I understand why. Abhinav hated Kras—'

'Or feared him,' Kalban cut in. 'That's a more accurate way of putting it.' He turned to Abhinav. 'You knew Kras didn't really support you for the throne. He just thought he'd be able to control you.'

'Let it *go*,' said Abhinav. 'I've already admitted it. If he'd been content to stay in retirement, I would have let him be. You have no reason to sound so superior. I saw the letter you wrote to him. You didn't make a secret of the fact that teaching Meenakshi Political Science was likely to be both frustrating and unprofitable—no offence intended,' Abhinav added to Meenakshi.

Meenakshi, who saw nothing offensive in the statement that she knew no Political Science, and, furthermore, wanted to know none, shrugged.

'I knew—yes, I *knew*—that you had some stupid idea of getting his sympathy, and Kras wouldn't be able to keep himself from getting involved. No matter what you believe, he wasn't going to aid in whatever plan you have to prove to people that you can rule.'

'Why did you want him dead, then? To help me? Do you expect anyone to believe that?'

'Of course I don't want to help you,' Abhinav snapped. 'I want the succession in my favour. I'm not *stupid*. I would be far better than you, and you know it.'

'Why? Because magic is evil?'

'Because you're ridiculous!' Abhinav threw up his hands. 'Ever since you came back, you've been moping in a corner because nobody is impressed that you can do a few spells. There's nothing wrong with magic. But you can't expect it to be *enough*.'

'Maybe you can discuss this later,' Meenakshi said, before Kalban could respond, and when it was clear that nobody else would intervene. 'Not in the middle of these people who are waiting for Chitralekha and me to leave so they can get on with regulating scorpion breeding.'

'We're waiting for Mada to leave, too,' said Rati. 'Preferably with prejudice, but that can wait. Finish your story.'

'There were other people with a reason to want Kras dead. Rati and Dev—yes, although they were using him.' Meenakshi turned to Rati. '*You* suspected that his allegiances were malleable. He was fond of Kalban—he always had been. He'd been willing to plot against him in his absence, but meeting Kalban again might have changed his mind.'

'*I* killed him?' Rati asked, still with a smile halfway between mirth and fondness, as though Meenakshi were a child making amusing mistakes while trying to read a volume of philosophy aloud. 'Is that your conclusion?'

'We considered it, but no. I don't think you knew that Mada was a Sprite and immune to poison. You wouldn't have wanted to kill *him*. Kalban was right about that. You do care about hurting innocent bystanders. Dev, by several accounts, went nowhere near Kras all evening. And I didn't see Dev taking that sort of risk.'

'We're in the clear. Good to hear.'

'Quite so,' said Meenakshi with a cryptic smile. 'Let me get back to blackmail. Amar provided us, very helpfully, with the information that Varo had been blackmailing Kras. Kras's participation in Angana's parents' attempt to depose the Prince had never been proved. Amar assumed Varo had proof. I suppose he did. Later, being the obliging person that he is, and wanting to make sure I didn't miss another potential suspect, Amar gave me a jewel that had belonged to Angana's family, telling me he'd found it in Varo's possession. That was a lie.'

'All the most shameless fabrication,' Varo said.

'Oh, no, not *all* of it. Persis pointed out to me that since it appeared that nearly everyone I came across had a motive to kill Kras, I should change my focus. It's astonishing how *accommodating* everyone's been. We went to Kras's house, where Angana, despite her grief, allowed us to look through his things. She said she hadn't touched them. We found a letter from Varo that was asking for something in exchange for silence.'

Varo stared at her. 'Perhaps you're not as much a fool as I thought you.'

'I don't read *people* well,' Meenakshi said. 'Letters, on the other hand, are no problem.'

'Even if I admit it—why would I have wanted to kill Kras if I was trying to get money from him? That sounds counterproductive.'

'That didn't make sense to me. Amar, who has been so eager to help us catch the murderer, pointed out to me that Kras might have had a change of heart and threatened to confess everything to the Prince. At his time of life, he had little to lose—but *you* have a great deal.'

'It's plausible, but your argument has one flaw. I didn't kill Kras.'

'I know you didn't.'

'It appears we're out of suspects? Unless you're suggesting that Kalban or Persis killed Kras. But in that case I assume your Dancer friend would have called in reinforcements, and possibly the Master Sorcerer.'

'We asked Persis where Amar had come from. She didn't know. I don't think she cared. She knew he'd come from one of the estates. It didn't much matter which, as long as he stayed loyal.

On the whole he *was* loyal to the Prince, he liked Abhinav—that was all right.'

'I'm gratified you think so,' said Amar.

'Of course, that brought up the question: why was Amar trying so hard to interfere? Angana asked me to investigate to get justice for her husband. That I could believe. I could also believe that Amar was willing to help direct me away from Abhinav out of friendship for him. But why was he trying so hard to convince me that Varo was a murderer?'

'Presumably because he didn't like Varo,' said Abhinav.

'I thought so, too, but he'd been chosen to be court bard because of his ability to get along with people, and he's known Varo for years without feeling the need to undermine him. Why would he risk his position at court now? That wasn't rational. There was one possible logical reason for Amar to want to prove Varo's guilt—that was to protect the true culprit.'

'So Amar killed Kras?' Persis asked, sceptical. 'Why?'

'Let me explain,' Chitralekha, said, taking up the story. 'We tried looking into Amar's background. We searched his room. We found a letter from his family. It was about loyalty to the Prince superseding loyalty to his own lord. That didn't make much sense, since Amar's family lived on a royal estate. So his liege lord was the Prince.' said Chitralekha, smiling at Amar's furious expression. 'Then why this urgent need to prove loyalty? Perhaps Amar's family had once rebelled against the Prince? Also unlikely, but not impossible.'

'Did your family rebel against me?' Shel asked Amar. 'I don't remember anything of the sort. It must have been many years ago. I hope I didn't punish them too harshly. We prefer to leave tenants alone as far as is feasible.'

'It *was* many years ago,' Meenakshi said. 'They were exiled.'

'But they wrote to him from the estate?'

Meenakshi glanced at Angana, whose eyes were blazing with an intensity that almost made her step back.

'Not Amar's family,' she said. 'Angana's.'

'Angana's family? I don't understand.'

'There must be thousands of people living on the royal estates. You wouldn't be expected to remember everyone. Amar came from Angana's family's estates—estates that were stripped from her father when he was convicted of sedition. They became part of the royal estates, but many of the tenants were still loyal to their original landlord—and to Angana, as his daughter, and the last member of the family still in Melucha. Amar wasn't going to let her be accused of murder . . . even if the accusation was true.'

'*Angana* killed Kras? Why? What reason had she to resent him? Or was she trying to get to me?'

'She meant no harm to you. She forgave you for exiling her family. She understood *that*. She wasn't aware of what had happened, that much was true. But she knew the price of sedition. She had no quarrel with you. What she *didn't* know was that Kras had had anything to do with it. You told me you took her evidence and had her sent away at once, so she wouldn't have to endure the trial.'

'I expect her friends didn't mention it to her,' Kalban went on. 'Out of compassion. She came back and married Kras, and people still didn't mention it to her—over time she saw less and less of her old friends and acquaintances. Soon, I expect, there were few around her who even knew.'

'We found Varo's letter,' Meenakshi held it up. 'Varo was very careful to protect himself. He didn't mention any names. He didn't say he was going to tell the *Prince* if Kras didn't pay him. When I spoke to the Prince and realized he had already guessed at Kras's involvement but didn't much care, I realized that Varo might have been speaking of someone else altogether.'

'But the thing that gave her away to us,' said Chitralekha, gesturing at the crate, 'was this.'

As one, the eyes of the Privy Council swivelled to it. It seemed they'd forgotten its existence.

'We found a secret chamber off Kalban's room,' Chitralekha went on. 'It contained a number of very old books about unpleasant forms of magic—don't worry, Meenakshi says they're inaccurate. They've been sent to the Master Sorcerer. We also found these.' She lifted out a couple of the jars to let the Council see the contents. 'Nothing illegal about them, but it was clear that someone had been interested in breeding venomous animals but had had to leave in a hurry. I admit I suspected Kalban at first, but Meenakshi said it didn't feel like his magic, or any magic, and she's unlikely to be wrong about that.'

'We thought it might have been Kras,' said Kalban.

'Or Abhinav,' Meenakshi said. 'Though, to be honest, I can't imagine Abhinav slaving under artificial light in a room with oozy walls.'

'I should hope not,' said Abhinav with a shudder.

'Someone released a dozen red scorpions into my room,' Meenakshi continued. 'Gopali was furious. She wanted to go home right away. It was difficult to talk her out of it. But whoever did that brought us closer to the answer. Kalban said red scorpions are difficult to get. Whoever had been breeding scorpions would have been able to get them—maybe she bred them herself.' Meenakshi glanced at Angana. 'You should have contented yourself with the vipers. Then I may never have made the connection. We went to the room to clear it out.'

'It was the books,' Kalban said. 'I suppose she kept them for sentimental reasons. Maybe her parents had brought them here, or she managed to get them out of the library on the estate. She should have burnt the lot. Even if the spells had been real, they would have been no good to her. But she couldn't bear to do it. We found the estate record book.'

'We got there eventually,' said Chitralekha. 'I think—although there's no way of being certain—that when Kras got Varo's letter, a few days before that dinner, he made a clean breast of things to his wife. His pension wasn't enough for him to pay the sums Varo expected, and Meenakshi was only staying a few months. He couldn't earn enough in that time.'

'She couldn't forgive him,' said Kalban. 'Kras had broken the trust invested in the position of Royal Tutor—and, worse in her eyes, he betrayed *her* trust. When Angana's family lost everything, when her parents and brother were forced to go to Vraja—maybe they sent her the red scorpions—Kras kept quiet about his part in things. He persuaded her to marry him—something she would never have done, had she known the whole truth. She couldn't forgive that.'

Angana's face was a stone mask.

'You've not explained how she did it,' Persis cut in. 'I, for one, would like to know.'

'It was the tea,' Meenakshi said. 'Angana didn't know there was some of Kras's tea still in the palace, much less that Abhinav had laced it with poison already. She packed a fresh supply for Kras to bring with him for the duration of his stay—and she probably went down and gave it to Mada, to make sure it would be used.'

'That's the truth,' Angana said.

'That was dangerous,' said Abhinav. 'Weren't you afraid of being caught?'

'She trusted that Amar would help her. And he did. And so did Mada . . . They ensured that the tea was returned along with the rest of Kras's possessions. It let her dispose of the evidence before we asked to look through Kras's things. The safety team had ensured that there was a very detailed inventory list. She did the best she could, in the circumstances. She threw away the tea and substituted dried ginger.'

'Very good.' Angana's smile was strained. 'You've thought of everything. But you've made one mistake. I was responsible for the scorpions in your room, but I don't know anything about any vipers.'

There was silence, broken by Kalban.

'Who's responsible for the vipers?' he demanded.

'What does it matter?' asked his father. 'They're just vipers. You must learn to curb this tendency to overreact.'

'Gopali will insist on leaving if I don't give her an answer.'

A movement caught his eye. He turned to look as his mother, whose expression of exasperated patience reminded him of the last time he'd seen it.

Oh.

'*You?*' he said, turning to Rati. 'Why?'

'Did you not realize I was planting them? Your mother knew before I did anything.' Rati turned to Persis. 'Do you see now? I know he's your son, but you can't pretend there's not a problem.'

'Explain,' Kalban demanded, before his mother could agree that there was a problem.

'I don't deny that the way we do things in Melucha is possibly not ideal,' Rati said, in the tone of one explaining the concept of treason to a toddler who ought, by now, to have learnt to distinguish it from sedition. 'Whatever our problems are, they're *our* problems. We are capable of solving them without outside assistance, as we've been doing through our history. But suddenly *you* were back, and we were inundated by Celestial Dancers. And Sprites,' she added, wrinkling her nose at Mada.

'How would killing Meenakshi have helped?'

'Don't be absurd. I wouldn't kill a *child*. I thought she could be relied upon to respond to unexpected danger in a picturesque manner. It would establish the need for changes—she's the daughter of the Lunatic of Madh.'

'He's not *that* bad,' protested Kalban.

'You say that because you've lived under his roof, in the City of the Insane, long enough to have absorbed the belief that making it rain on people trying to have dinner in peace is a legitimate method of dispute resolution. Had Meenakshi reacted to the threat as I expected, it would have justified stricter measures against unauthorized magic.'

'And that would have justified *you* in trying to have me sent away.'

'Meenakshi surprised me,' said Rati. 'She didn't overreact.'

'I didn't dare,' said Meenakshi. 'Kalban would never have let me hear the end of it.'

'That's a point in his favour. We all have things to reevaluate, including the place of magic in Melucha and Kalban's fitness to rule. One day you will be Governor of the Southern Provinces of Pür. Kalban may or may not be Prince of Melucha. Before you use flocks of Harpies as an argument in a dispute over territorial waters–'

'Madh is landlocked.'

'The border across the mountains–'

'We don't have a common border.'

'Before you use flocks of Harpies as an argument in a dispute over any issue that, not being a soothsayer, I can't think of now, it comes as a relief to know that you seem willing to listen to reason from Kalban. I'll keep that in mind. I expect Persis will say she could have told me as much if I'd asked her.'

'Am I supposed to thank her?' Meenakshi asked Kalban.

'*No.* Just get on with it.'

'Where were we? Oh, yes, the hemlock in the tea. *You*,' she said, turning on Mada, 'did nothing. Abhinav was a child when he put the hemlock in the tea. Angana had been left alone in the world, torn from everything she knew. She had rebuilt her life and had just heard something terrible and wasn't in her right mind. *They're* both human. *You're* supposed to be better than this.'

Mada turned to her as though about to argue, but something in her eyes cowed him.

'We'll deal with him,' Chitralekha said.

'I don't want to see him in the Mortal Realm again.'

'You won't.'

'What I don't understand,' Kalban said to Angana, 'is why you went and *asked* Meenakshi to investigate.'

'Don't you? I hoped to direct her thoughts towards Rati, who seemed a *much* likelier candidate. I'm sure there are half a dozen murders to her name of which she's not been proven guilty.'

'If I've not been proven guilty,' said Rati, 'then they're not to my name.

'As long as Mada kept my secret,' Angana went on, 'you would have no reason to suspect me, not with Rati flaunting her aims and her palace informants.' She paused, looking suddenly so fierce that Kalban took an involuntary step back. 'Do you think it didn't occur to me to read Kras's letters before I let you look at his things? I *wanted* his actions to be known.'

'Let me interject,' said Rati. Kalban felt gruding respect: he wouldn't have dared address Angana. 'We *knew*. Everyone old enough to remember your family knew that, even if it was never proven, Kras had been involved with their attempted coup—'

'And you did *nothing*. My parents and brother were impoverished and exiled—a just punishment perhaps, but what was Kras's just punishment for the same crime—and for keeping it secret from me all these years? I lost *everything*.' The look she cast Rati was so dark Kalban expected her to burst into flames. 'I would have been one of the highest-ranking members of the Privy Council, and I had to give way to pretentious little upstarts—'

'If you're calling me an upstart,' Dev snarled.

Shel cleared his throat. Silence fell like a cloak.

'Sympathetic as I am to the many and varied emotions you must feel,' he said, 'I recommend that you discuss slights to your personal honour outside the council chamber. Meenakshi, please continue.'

'There's not much else,' Meenakshi said. 'Angana took it on herself to mete out justice.'

'Yes. I did. Nobody else was going to do it for me.' Angana turned to the Prince. 'Now you know the truth. I was hoping to avoid it, but I'm not afraid of a trial. I have nothing to hide.'

'I don't think that will be necessary,' Shel said. 'You've confessed before several witnesses. A trial would be unpleasant and have no practical benefit.' He paused. 'We try to be open minded, but . . . You'll agree that there must be consequences for this.'

EPILOGUE

'And after that,' Meenakshi muttered, glowering at the stack of books next to her, 'I *still* have to write the essays.'

'You didn't think you were getting out of it?' asked Kalban, amused. 'Angana was happy to have her jewel back, by the way. She asked me to thank you.'

'I thought Varo would be dismissed as a blackmailer.'

'He's lost his seat on the Privy Council,' said Kalban. 'He might still cherish a hope of becoming Royal Tutor someday, but we can agree *that's* hardly a prize. This is Melucha. You aren't disgraced for having blackmailed a political rival with your knowledge of his complicity in a plot against the throne. You *are* punished for being stupid enough to be found out, which Varo has been.'

The door to Kalban's study opened, admitting Chitralekha.

'I came to say goodbye,' she announced, as she pulled a chair up to the round table where Meenakshi and Kalban sat. 'I'm closing the investigation this afternoon and submitting my report to Rambha. Unless she has any follow-up questions, which I don't anticipate, I won't be coming back to Melucha in a hurry.'

'What's happening to Mada?'

Chitralekha's smile could have rivalled the sun. 'Oh, he's had it. He got found out—and he allowed himself to be compromised. It'll be centuries before he can work himself into favour again.'

'I still don't understand that,' said Meenakshi, pushing aside the sheet of paper on which she had, after two hours of work, inscribed a title and subtitle. 'Why *did* he conceal Angana's part in it? And why didn't he prevent it from happening in the first place? I don't buy his explanation.'

'I had a word with him about that. Angana appealed to him personally.'

'How? He couldn't have seen Angana before that day.'

'That's when she spoke to him.' Chitralekha cast a sidelong glance at Kalban. 'Mada said nobody was paying much attention to either of them.'

Kalban grimaced. 'That's true. I never thought of it upsetting Angana so much. I should have. Maybe she wouldn't have done it.'

'If it makes you feel better, I don't think you could have saved Kras. Once Angana found out about his involvement in the plot that led to her family's banishment and her own loss of power, she made up her mind. Anyway, Mada claims he felt sorry for Angana, but I think he saw the opportunity at once. If he could persuade Rambha and Urvashi that *you* were responsible for the death—'

'He'd get a promotion?' Kalban asked bitterly. 'I hope you're at least going to be careful whom you send here in future.'

'It wasn't only you he was after. Once I was put in charge of the investigation, he was also trying to impede me. He wanted me to have to go back and admit that he was right—or, better yet, to come to some conclusion that he could easily disprove.'

'I hope you realize that Mada would have caused more harm than good if he'd had his way. It would have been a disaster—just when there's a hope of persuading people in Melucha that magic isn't dangerous.'

'It would have been unfortunate for you, but you know Rambha doesn't care about mortal politics as long as it doesn't become a problem for us—but, yes, I agree,' Chitralekha added hastily. 'The watchful integration strategy might require more work. At the very least we should send someone more senior, even to low-concentration locations.'

'It seems terrible,' Meenakshi said, 'that Kras is dead and in the end . . . it makes less difference than Mada's attempt to incriminate Kalban. Angana will be exiled, but there's nothing left for her in Melucha *anyway* and she'll probably go to her family wherever they are. Varo loses his Privy Council seat but may still get the sinecure he's angling for.'

'Varo didn't kill Kras.'

'He might as well have done. If he hadn't blackmailed him, Angana might never have . . . No, that's wrong,' Meenakshi said. 'People are responsible for what they've done. Kras *should* have told her the truth. He was wrong to keep it from her. Varo was wrong to blackmail him. Angana was *very* wrong to kill him.'

'Things aren't always clear-cut,' said Chitralekha. 'Sometimes, like in this case, there's an unpleasant situation that, given time, *might* resolve itself. Sometimes the unpleasant situation is brought to an abrupt and unfortunate end.'

'And so we pretend nothing bad happened? Kras is *dead*. It's not just an *unpleasant* situation.'

'It's *over*. We know the truth. My work isn't about *punishment*. It's about preventing bad things from happening. We've done that. Angana is free, but she isn't likely to be a threat to anyone else. Varo bears some share of blame, I agree. That happens. Maybe one of the things you have to learn while you're here is that you can't always expect a perfect solution. Life isn't a play. Sometimes people who've done something wrong get off. Sometimes people who *haven't* done any wrong suffer.'

There was a short rap at the door.

'Are you expecting anyone?' Chitralekha asked.

'No.' Kalban opened the door. 'Oh. You. I should have known.'

'I'm delighted to see you too. I won't wait for you to ask me in.' Abhinav strode past Kalban. 'Family shouldn't stand on ceremony.'

'What do you want?'

'I'm not here for an argument.' Abhinav glanced around the room. 'I hope I haven't walked into the middle of one. I'd hate to be caught in the crossfire.'

'There's no crossfire. We're not *children*.' Meenakshi waved at the chair by the window, which slid smoothly across the floor to Abhinav. 'Why don't you sit? *What?*' she added, when she caught Kalban's glare. 'You're always telling me to be more courteous.'

'Don't worry.' Abhinav looked between Meenakshi and Chitralekha. Evidently he decided that, despite the evidence of the self-propelling chair, Meenakshi was the lesser evil, because he slid the chair between hers and Kalban's. 'I'm not going to run screaming. Why are you still standing there, Kalban? It's terribly rude to wait by the door like you're anticipating my departure.'

'What do you want?' Kalban said again.

'I never thought you'd killed Kras.'

'That's clear,' Meenakshi pointed out, 'considering that you thought *you'd* killed him.'

'Has anyone ever told you strict factual accuracy isn't always desirable?'

'The Head of the Inter-Realm Liaison Bureau, several times.'

'Oh, good. I was just curious. It's not a compliment to Kalban. I didn't think he was capable of doing it. I still don't. He's not. This is something you need to realize. It's why you have a hard time fitting in,' he added to his brother.

'You're scared of magic but you consider it a virtue to murder people?' Meenakshi asked.

'Of course it's not a virtue,' Abhinav said. 'It's a very inefficient way of settling problems. But, if you'll excuse my honesty, it's just as inefficient to have so much unregulated magic that some of the most powerful magicians in Madh have to devote their energies to making sure other magicians don't end the world. Humans tend to be inefficient.'

'And I'm inefficient in the wrong way, I suppose,' said Kalban, abandoning his post by the door and reseating himself.

'You scare people. There's no point in pretending otherwise. And this is exactly what I didn't want. I *said* I'm not here to argue.' Abhinav paused. 'I'm here to tell you we don't need to bicker like this all the time.'

'You mean you're not going to object if I take the throne?'

'Not *that*,' said Abhinav. 'I have a lot of objections to your taking the throne, prime among them being that I'm far better qualified. But it'll be years before we have to worry about that and in the meantime we needn't try to kill each other. And you shouldn't try to hide your magic so much, at least not at home. That's why you're so jumpy and miserable.'

'You just said I'm scaring people.'

'Because you're jumpy! Mother used to turn people into pigs and people are less worried about her! I'm not saying you should go *that* far, but if you want to brew potions or whatever it is you do, here in the palace, do it. I won't use it against you.'

'Oh.' Kalban paused. 'Thank you?'

Abhinav shrugged. 'She's my mother, too. I may not be able to *do* magic, but I'm not scared of it. If you have any sense, you'll use the time Meenakshi's here to show other people that there's no reason to be scared. Stop hiding her—and yourself—in the palace. That just makes people think there's something not right. There's no more Section 39.'

He got to his feet.

'You're leaving?' Chitralekha asked.

'I said what I came to say.'

'Are you friends now?' Meenakshi asked, when the door had closed behind Abhinav.

'I suppose you could say,' said Kalban, 'that we're no longer enemies.'

As a child, Aditi greatly enjoyed sports and once outswam a porpoise. She later had a chequered career that included working as a pet food taster. In her downtime, she enjoys long-distance running and partying with her friends on Friday nights.

Just kidding. It's all fiction, just like the rest of this book.

Read the opening of *The Magicians of Madh*, the first book in the series.

The streets of Madh, even in the middle of the night, were a beehive of activity.

In any other city of the Free Lands, this would never have been tolerated by the authorities. The odd passer-by or late reveller is one thing. No self-respecting Captain of the Guard wants to look out over his city under a gibbous moon and see alleys and byways bursting with potential troublemakers.

The streets of Madh were a beehive of activity, not because the Guardsmen of Madh were more tolerant than their counterparts in Khand, Sala or Vraja. It was because the multitude thronging those streets in the small hours consisted of not just humans but also Sprites, nagas, daemons, djinn and all manner of spirits from the Realm between Realms. One of the indispensable qualities of a good Captain of the Guard is the ability to know when to enforce discipline and when to retreat into the watchtower and bar the door. Failure to appreciate this difference might turn a noisy but peaceful crowd into a screaming mob of looters.

Every city has a focus, one point around which the tide of life eddies and swirls. In Madh, this focus was the Royal Academy of Science, Magic and the Arts, whose golden domes, despite being shorter than the tops of the buildings surrounding them, dominated the skyline.

It was towards the Academy that two men were weaving their way.

The first, who drew the eye, was clad in a blue robe. He was human—undeniably, earthily human—and imposing. He was nearly a foot taller than everybody else, and proportionately wide. Most of his mass seemed to consist of rippling muscle, though the folds of his blue robe were so bulky that one could only guess.

What people *could* see was that slung over his left shoulder was a great war bow even taller than he was. A quiver bristling with arrows was strapped to his back.

People made way for the man. Priests made way for him. Guards made way for him. Even djinn made way for him. Once he had passed, people, priests, guards and djinn all looked away.

None of them spotted the grey-robed man padding in his wake.

The men walked past the Academy to Temple Square.

It was called Temple *Square* because that had been the original intent. It was really more of a lopsided dodecagon. Nobody knew why. The temples themselves were marvels of precision engineering. It was inconceivable that a culture that had used sticks and shadows for measurement and maintained a margin of error below half of one tenth of one percent could have failed to draw four straight lines joined at four right angles. Tour guides told romantic stories involving forbidden love, powerful enchantresses and the sculpture of the six-legged horse on the façade of the Sun Temple. The truth, of course, was far more mundane and far less interesting, and is therefore irrelevant to this story.

The two men picked their way to a small cluster of sculptures in the centre of the Square. The man in grey approached the statue of the God of Watchful Peace, who presided over the revelry with unnerving obsidian eyes.

'Well? We're here.' The man in grey didn't whisper. A whisper would have been conspicuous. He bellowed, and his raised voice was lost in the cacophony of all the other raised voices.

All the same, somebody must have heard, because a moment later, a response issued from somewhere in the region of the elephant on the god's shield. Nobody other than the two men paid it attention; the inhabitants of Madh were as accustomed to strange voices as people in other cities were accustomed to sparrows in the eaves.

'You were to come alone,' said the voice. It should have sounded sinister and foreboding, with a vague overshadow of menace. But it was the sort of unmemorable voice that could have belonged to the assistant under-accountant of a merchant barely breaking even; it only sounded petulant.

The grey-robed man responded accordingly.

'I *am* alone. Chanura is my eyes and ears. And my hands, when I need it. As you may be aware, I no longer involve myself in . . . implementation.'

'All right.' There was a pause for thought, before the voice went on, this time achieving a monotone that betrayed no emotion but was still too ordinary to be eerie. 'I have something important that must be done. I know you have a reputation for efficient fieldwork, but I require a high degree of finesse. We can discuss payment after you've understood the nature of the assignment.'

The voice spoke. The men listened. Around them, the crowd thinned as the night turned to morning.